HOLLY, JOLLY, AND OH SO NAUGHTY

AVA GRAY

Copyright © 2024 by Ava Gray

All rights reserved.

No part of this book may be reproduced in any form or by any electronic or mechanical means, including information storage and retrieval systems, without written permission from the author, except for the use of brief quotations in a book review.

❦ Created with Vellum

ALSO BY AVA GRAY

CONTEMPORARY ROMANCE
Mafia Kingpins Series

His to Own

His to Protect

His to Win

The Valkov Bratva Series

Stolen by the Bratva

Kept by the Bratva

Captured by the Bratva

Festive Flames Series

Silver Hills' Christmas Miracle

AVA GRAY

Holly, Jolly, and Oh So Naughty

Harem Hearts Series

3 SEAL Daddies for Christmas

Small Town Sparks

Her Protector Daddies

Her Alpha Bosses

The Mafia's Surprise Gift

The Billionaire Mafia Series

Knocked Up by the Mafia

Stolen by the Mafia

Claimed by the Mafia

Arranged by the Mafia

Charmed by the Mafia

Alpha Billionaire Series

Secret Baby with Brother's Best Friend

Just Pretending

Loving The One I Should Hate

Billionaire and the Barista

Coming Home

Doctor Daddy

Baby Surprise

A Fake Fiancée for Christmas

Hot Mess

Love to Hate You - The Beckett Billionaires

Just Another Chance - The Beckett Billionaires

Valentine's Day Proposal

The Wrong Choice - Difficult Choices

The Right Choice - Difficult Choices

SEALed by a Kiss

The Boss's Unexpected Surprise

Twins for the Playboy

When We Meet Again

The Rules We Break

Secret Baby with my Boss's Brother

Frosty Beginnings

Silver Fox Billionaire

Taken by the Major

Daddy's Unexpected Gift

Off Limits

Boss's Baby Surprise

CEO's Baby Scandal

Playing with Trouble Series:

Chasing What's Mine

Claiming What's Mine

Protecting What's Mine

Saving What's Mine

The Beckett Billionaires Series:

Love to Hate You

Just Another Chance

Standalone's:

Ruthless Love

The Best Friend Affair

PARANORMAL ROMANCE

Maple Lake Shifters Series:

Omega Vanished

Omega Exiled

Omega Coveted

Omega Bonded

Everton Falls Mated Love Series:

The Alpha's Mate

The Wolf's Wild Mate

Saving His Mate

Fighting For His Mate

Dragons of Las Vegas Series:

Thin Ice

Silver Lining

A Spark in the Dark

Fire & Ice

Dragons of Las Vegas Boxed Set (The Complete Series)

Standalone's:

Fiery Kiss

Wild Fate

BLURB

Daddy, it's Christmas...

Seven years ago, I had a steamy fling with a gorgeous med student.

Three weeks of pure bliss.

He set my heart on fire.

I thought we had something real.

Then he vanished without a trace.

Now he's back in my small town.

Walking into my parents' inn like he owns the place.

Looking even more delicious than I remember.

And he needs a fake girlfriend.

God, what was I thinking saying yes?

Now we're playing couple at charity events.

Getting snowed in at my bakery.

Making out like teenagers under the mistletoe.

Creating memories that feel dangerously real.

His touch still sets me ablaze.

His kisses still make me weak.

But I've got a secret bigger than Santa's gift list...

Our six-year-old daughter.

The same daughter who just called him "Daddy" at the Christmas festival.

In front of everyone.

The same daughter I never told him about.

Now he's storming out into the snow.

Leaving me and our daughter behind.

Again.

Will this Christmas miracle end in heartbreak?

Or will Santa finally deliver the family we've always dreamed of?

Sometimes the best presents come wrapped in secrets...

And second chances come with a price.

Author's Note: A steamy small-town Christmas romance featuring a single mom, a secret baby, fake dating, and a doctor who never stopped loving the one who got away.

1

LILY

REMINDER: *The annual Christmas Day Daddy/Daughter dance will be held at the Town Hall this year, not the School.*

The crimson words glare up at me from a nauseating green poster, and my stomach flips slightly. Each year, the daddy/daughter dance comes around like a beacon, reminding me of the very thing my darling daughter Emma doesn't have.

A father.

At least not one who's in her life to take her to such a dance. I've skillfully dodged questions each year, and Emma's been happy to attend the dance with her grandfather, but she's six now, and the questions become clearer. More demanding.

I'm not sure how much longer I can keep the truth from her when fairy tales are quickly losing their sparkle.

How do I tell my child that she doesn't have a father because he never wanted her? How do I tell her that while her room is filled with books about happy families?

I don't have the strength to tell her when she looks up at me with her gigantic blue eyes.

Beyond the corkboard filled with announcements for all unsuspecting parents, activity in the classroom just beyond the closed door takes my attention. Emma is inside, engrossed in an animated conversation with a friend who seemingly enjoys the taste of plastic animals. Emma's curls fly back and forth as she dramatically shakes her head, and laughter pulls from my chest.

"She's adorable," says a voice to my left.

I turn to face a man dressed in a light blue shirt and a cream sweater. He flashes me a bright smile and adjusts his oval spectacles while glancing past me into the classroom.

"You know which one is mine?"

"Emma, right? You're Lily Thompson, unless I'm embarrassingly mistaken."

"No, no, you're right." I smile back, taking in his brown curls and the dusting of powdered chalk along his sleeves. "And you are?"

"Mr. Sepher." He holds out one pale hand. "Mark. Please."

"Nice to meet you, Mark." Taking his hand, I notice there's an odd dryness to his palm that immediately sends a scratchy sensation up my arm, but his grip is warm and firm.

"The pleasure is all mine." He locks eyes with me, and the handshake lingers until I flex my fingers for release.

"Is your kid in there?" I tilt my head toward the classroom and quickly glance at the clock. I'm not typically this early, but time was on my side today, and there are still a few minutes until the bell rings to release the hoards of children kept safe inside these walls.

"Oh, no, I have none of my own," Mark says with a soft laugh. "I teach here. In fact, I think Emma will be in my class next year. How about that?"

"Oh, that's nice!" My smile wavers a fraction. It's only November, and Emma still has half a year left in her current grade. "I didn't realize they sorted things like that so early."

"What can I say? We're incredibly efficient here." Then he winks at me. "And caring."

I nod politely, sneaking another glance at the clock.

This town is small, and in some ways, everyone knows everyone else. While I run one of the most popular bakeries in town and participate in almost every event hosted throughout the year, I try to avoid making small talk because I simply don't have the patience for it.

Who cares what the weather is like or how much the price of fertilizer has increased at the grocer?

"Is Emma excited?" Mark reaches up and peels the daddy/daughter dance poster off the wall. "For the dance?"

"Yup. Just like every other six-year-old. She sees it as some special party for her on Christmas Day which just makes everything a little more special, y'know?"

"I can imagine." Mark taps his fingers against the paper and then clears his throat. "And her father?"

There it is, that daunting question from anyone who only knows me in passing. They carry the same assumption that everyone else does the moment they meet Emma, though I can't really blame them. Maybe I'd be guilty of the same if my situation were any different.

"She dances with her grandfather," I reply. It's a non-answer, but I'll leave it to Mark to fill in the gaps.

"Ah." Mark's tone lifts and he taps the poster again. "Not the sort of thing you would take a boyfriend to, I'd imagine."

Is he... trying to flirt with me?

I smile wider, trying to maintain a polite air as the clock drags its hand toward the hour mark. "I don't have a boyfriend. And even if I did, I wouldn't have him attend something like that. It's for family, y'know?"

"Sure," Mark says, pressing the poster back onto the board. "But a boyfriend can become family."

"True." I laugh softly. "I'd need to get one first."

Mark suddenly straightens up next to me, and when he faces me, he's a few inches closer than he was before.

Is this really happening?

"You run that bakery in town, don't you? What's it called, Sweetest something?"

"*Sweet Noel,*" I correct him quickly. "Cliché, I know, but I opened at Christmas and my festive designs always get the biggest surge of attention online, so it's fitting."

This is good. I can talk about business and baking until I'm hoarse and whoever is listening is bored stiff. Baking wasn't my initial passion when I entered the culinary world. I had dreams of becoming a top chef at some fancy restaurant where people would spend their house down payments on one of my steaks. But college had different ideas for me and from my first cake decorating class, I was hooked.

Spending my evenings up to my elbows in marzipan isn't as glamorous as a fancy, rich steakhouse in the city, but it's definitely more enjoyable.

"No judgment from me." Mark lifts both his hands, palms upward. "Half this town is named after something Christmassy. Even that crazy old Inn, *Fir Tree*? The food is good, but the name?"

I snort softly. "Oh, my parents' inn?"

"Your parents'?" Mark's face loses a few shades. "When—when I say crazy, I just mean in a kooky sort of way, y'know, like something out of a postcard."

Whether fate wanted to save me from the conversation or Mark from his embarrassment, I couldn't be sure, but as those words left Mark's lips, a sudden yell rose up from down the hall. Two kids quickly became engaged in a small brawl over who was the owner of the silver coat.

"Shouldn't you…?" I raise a brow and tilt my head in their direction. Mark's relief is clear as he makes excuses and quickly hurries after the quarreling children.

In his absence, my next breath shifts easier in my chest. I can't fault him for trying to take an interest in me. The dating pool in this town is rather limited, but dating is far from my mind.

My heart still, painfully, belongs to one man, and I've yet to draw it out of his grasp.

James Anderson was a handsome, brilliant man who blew onto my college campus for a medical seminar with his father, and he blew right into my heart. As a small-town girl, there was something so beautifully intimidating about people who lived their lives in the spotlight of the city, and James was exactly that. His father was famous in the medical world, to a degree, and he was next in line.

He was funny and kind, so incredibly sweet and attentive, and the sex was… I adjust my stance and pull lightly at the collar of my blouse. He completely stole my heart.

And then he left as quickly as he arrived, leaving me heartbroken and confused.

And pregnant.

I tried for weeks to get in touch with him to tell him he was going to be a father, but the only person I was able to reach was his mother.

Turns out his sweetness was all an act and he was the kind of asshole who got his mother to break bad news. He didn't want to see me, didn't want to hear from me. I was an easily forgotten fling and nothing more. That didn't change even when I told his mother I was pregnant.

Her response still haunts me to this day.

My eyes close, and I swallow down the ache of old hurt that threatens to rise at the memory. James made himself clear, so I honored his wishes.

I never contacted him again.

That doesn't stop me from looking him up on social media after one too many glasses of wine, but he's been inactive for years. Some nights, it's hard to believe he was even real.

"Mommy!" Emma's bright, happy voice bursts through the air and immediately pulls me out of my dark thought spiral. I'd been so caught up in memory lane that I didn't even hear the bell I yearned for.

"Hi, darling!" I open my eyes and crouch just in time for my daughter to barrel into my arms with an excited cry. She hugs me with all her might, not caring for how the strap of her rucksack smacks me in the mouth or how her folder stabs me in the stomach.

All she wants is a hug.

"Mommy, Mommy, you'll never guess!" Emma bounces around excitedly as I stand and take her rucksack from her shoulders.

"What is it?" I ask her, quickly waving goodbye to Amelia, her teacher and my best friend. Taking her fist in my hand, we walk down the hallway toward the doors, weaving between the sea of children and parents, all sharing that after-school moment.

"I got three gold stars today!" Emma's so excited that she can barely keep still.

"That's amazing!"

When we make it to the steps, she pulls her hand away from mine and comically stomps down each step to the bottom. Once there, she pauses and holds out her hand.

"Come on, Mommy," she says matter-of-factly as if my descent is holding her up.

"I'm here, I'm here. Okay, tell me. What did you get the stars for?"

"I got one for my reading." Emma counts it out on her hand with her pink folder tucked under one arm. "One for helping Katie with her knee because she fell in the playground, but I got her up and helped her inside. And one for feeding the fish!"

"Aww, Emma. That's brilliant! I'm proud of you, sweetie."

"I know!" Emma continues her stomping as we walk toward my car.

"Why are you walking like that?"

"Like what?" She glances innocently up at me.

"Like this." Holding her rucksack up, I mimic her stomping steps until she squeals and pushes into me.

"Mommy, stop!" Emma giggles. "You're not doing it right!"

"Okay, then how am I supposed to do it? And why are you doing it?"

"Because." Emma stops abruptly and places one hand on her waist. "*Because* Mrs. Grant said that powerful walking is a good way to confed—confrid… confiderence!"

It's becoming hard to hold in my laughter. "Do you mean confidence?"

"Yeah!" Emma resumes her stompy walking and it suddenly clicks for me. Emma may have taken the *powerful* walking tip literally.

"Is it working? Do you feel confident?"

"Yeah!" Emma declares as we reach my car. "I need it 'cause… 'cause Keiran and his friend Martin were being mean to me today."

"Wait, what?" My heart drops to my gut. "What happened?"

"It's nothin'," Emma says casually, pulling open the car door. I help her inside, and as I'm clipping her into her booster seat, I lock eyes with her.

"If they're being mean to you, sweetie, we can do something about it, okay?"

"You can't," Emma says, and she pats my cheek with one small hand. "Only Daddy can!"

A chill whips down my spine. "What?"

"They said–they said that they don't believe I had a dad an' that's why Grandpa always comes to the dance. I told them I do and that he's just away, like you say." Emma sniffles and settles into her seat. "They don't believe me 'cause they never seen him, but I told them I'm gonna ask him this year and this year, he can come with me, right, Mommy?"

She stares up at me with such an intense innocence that my heart breaks.

"Emma…"

"You can call him, right? I told them you would."

"I…" I can't say it. Not like this, huddled in the back of the car with a seatbelt catching on my arm and the exhaustion of the day weighing down on me. "Sure, baby. I can call him."

It looks like my years of telling her fairy tales are finally over.

2

JAMES

"Are you sure about this?" The woman in my chair continues tearing her soggy tissues into confetti strips while sniffling. "What if it doesn't work?"

It's impossible to keep my heart out of situations like this. As a gynecologist, I see people at their most vulnerable, and facing a woman who has been trying to have children for years to no avail doesn't get any easier.

"Samantha, with any treatment, there is always a chance it won't work," I reply as gently as I can. "And I have to remind you that this isn't any kind of miracle injection. If you choose to go down this route, then it will be expensive and incredibly taxing on your mental and emotional health."

"But I could have a baby?" She lifts her swimming eyes to me, and the sadness pouring out of her shoots me straight in the chest.

"Yes. With IVF, it definitely increases your chances."

She breaks down once again, sobbing into her hands. I lean back and collect some fresh, dry tissues then press them into her palms.

"I always…" She sniffles and hiccups. "I always thought there was something wrong with me!"

"No," I assure her. "There's nothing wrong, per se. Your body is just different and needs some help. But I stress that you must talk this over with your partner, okay? You cannot make this decision alone, and it will be a long road."

Samantha nods through her tears, trying to stifle her sobs. "Thank you, Doctor. Thank you!"

The thanks feels too early since I haven't done anything other than go over her test results and offer her some options, but they are options that didn't exist in this town until I got here, so her overwhelming gratitude is understandable.

"It's no problem. Now, I don't feel right sending you away like this so come with me, if you don't mind?"

Samantha nods. When she stands, her legs are trembling so I quickly wrap an arm around her shoulders and guide her out of my room and into the reception area.

"Taylor, could you get Mrs. Hill a hot cup of tea, please, and bring it to the break room?"

My receptionist, Taylor, leaps to action immediately and hurries over to the coffee room while I guide Samantha into the staff room and sit her down on the couch.

"Now, Samantha. I want you to stay here and drink some tea until you feel better, okay? And once you're calm, Taylor will call you a taxi to take you home, okay?"

"Oh." Samantha weeps and she pats my arm. "You don't have to do that. It's too much."

"Think nothing of it," I assure her. Taylor arrives right on cue with a steaming hot cup of tea. Taking it, I hand it to Samantha and squeeze her shoulder. "Drink. Slowly. It will help."

"What did you do?" Taylor hisses to me out of the side of her mouth as we stop near the door.

"I just gave her some options," I reply. "Options I think she either never knew about or had written off long ago."

"You know, if you keep making the patients cry, someone's gonna think we're doing something wrong."

"Don't worry." I clasp Taylor's shoulder. "They're happy tears. I think. Can you keep an eye on her? Call her a taxi when she's ready to leave? I'll pay. I don't mind."

Taylor rolls her eyes. "An Angel this close to Christmas? Careful or they'll rope you into the Nativity show next."

With a laugh, I leave Taylor and Samantha alone and return to my office.

Closing my door, I breathe deeply and close my eyes.

It never gets old. No matter how many people sit before me with health concerns and more, delivering good or bad news doesn't get any easier. These poor souls look at me like I hold their life in my hands.

Once upon a time, I thought it was something I would get numb to. I would watch my father attend his conferences and speak about people in such a detached way. As one of the country's leading surgeons, maybe he taught himself to disconnect, but I always assumed it would be something that would come naturally.

Last year, I would have said I was well on my way to emotionally detaching from my patients.

Then, my father passed suddenly three months ago, and everything felt raw. Like I'd been skinned alive and left as just this raw, painful nerve absorbing the agony of everyone around me.

Returning to my desk, I sit down heavily in my chair and sigh as a familiar wave of grief rushes through me like a burst of static. I may not have learned to emotionally detach like my father, but I certainly grasped his idea of running away.

My childhood was filled with verbal fights between my parents that would only be resolved by my father disappearing to some out-of-state work or a conference. Then he would return with flowers and an apology, and it would be peaceful until the next fight.

I fled.

My father's death was a wake-up call to the smothering life I found myself trapped in. From the day I was born, my mother had everything planned out for me, from my schooling to my career path and then my fiancée.

Ex-fiancée.

I left the ring and an apology note on her bedside table three months ago and never looked back because losing my father highlighted one very hidden truth in my heart.

I didn't love my fiancée because I was in love with another. I always had been, and there simply wasn't enough space in my heart for anyone else.

Leaning forward, all it takes are a few key taps to bring up the website for this town's famous bakery, the *Sweet Noel,* run by the gorgeous Lily Thompson.

The woman who has my heart.

Maybe it's the grief talking. Maybe I'm crazy.

Packing up and ditching my life within one night to come halfway across the country to a state I've never been in, just for a glimpse of the woman I've been in love with for seven years.

A woman I was forced to forget due to family obligations.

In my few months in Silver Hills, I've expertly avoided her other than a few walks past her bakery seeking just a glimpse. I'm surely nothing more than a distant memory to her, but right now, with my life a mess and my heart broken, she's the medicine I need.

Bringing my expertise to a town like this has the added benefit of making me feel like I can still do good things.

I know the *Sweet Noel* website by heart and yet I still take my time scrolling through the pages until I reach the 'About Us' section. Lily's smiling face shines above an award for best confectionary three years running. The sight of her makes my heart swell and I—

"James, why on earth is Mrs. Hill sobbing her heart out in the staff room?"

My door bursts open and my boss, Margret, stands in the doorway with her arms crossed and her small, rectangular glasses perched on the tip of her nose.

I quickly close the *Sweet Noel* page and heat warms my face and neck as if I've just been caught looking at something naughty, like a teenager caught by their parents.

"Uhm… I gave her some unexpected good news. Not even good news, just hopeful news, I think, and it hit her harder than she expected. Than either of us expected." I shift in my seat, still flushed.

"Hmm. Well, that had better be all. This place had a nice reputation before you started here."

"Has your reputation suffered?"

"No," Margret replies stiffly, "but we don't need people seeing a stream of sobbing women leaving your office."

"Well…" I snort softly. "When you put it like that…"

"And another thing." Margret strides forward and rounds my desk.

When her eyes flit to my computer screen, I'm infinitely grateful I closed that window. "You need to do something about this."

"About what?" I scan her quickly and my eyes lock onto the phone in her hand.

"About this!" She thrusts the device toward me, and my heart sinks.

A few button presses and there's a flood of missed calls and voicemails from two numbers I instantly recognize. My mother and my ex-fiancée.

"Your mom and your fiancée—"

"Ex-fiancée," I correct sharply.

"Ex-fiancée are still calling non-stop, blocking up the line to actual patients. You told me you would handle this."

"I believe I said I was *handling* it," I correct her again, quickly deleting all the voicemails. There's nothing either of them can say that I want to hear. "As in, I'm in the process."

"James." Margret perches on the edge of my desk and adjusts her glasses although they never shift from the small indent on the tip of her nose. The beaded chain that runs from the leg of her glasses to her cardigan tinkles at the movement and momentarily distracts me.

Margret is exactly how I pictured her when I called her months ago inquiring about the position here. Her nasally voice has a rough edge to it, created from the cigarettes I knew she used to smoke daily. She doesn't anymore, but her fingers are always twiddling with a pen or something similar and she pops hard candy mints like they're going out of fashion. Even now, she sits there toying with those beads to keep her fingers busy. She smiles at me, deepening the wrinkles on her face and giving her an oddly charming look despite her brash personality.

She's a woman who has seen it all over the years but still has a smile to take home to her family. Sure, she can be as sour as the bitterest lemon at the end of fall, but she has a good heart. A good heart that's clearly at the end of its tether from the narrow-eyed look she's giving me.

"We're a family-owned business," Margret says.

My heart plummets.

"Having a big shot from the city makes us look good, and despite the tears you draw out of the patients, you're doing good work here. Work I never thought a practice like ours could ever achieve. But even I have my limits." Margret takes the phone from me and taps the screen. "We're a Medical Practice, not a call center. Now, I've given you your privacy, and I have done my best not to ask why a hot-shot doctor like you decided to move to a small town like Evergreen Falls, but we can't keep this up. It's becoming more trouble than it might be worth."

"What are you saying?" I press my fingertips into my thigh, fighting against a lump rising in my throat. I can already see where this is going. If it's too much hassle to employ me, then I'll be out on my ear, and what then? What other excuse do I have to stay here trying to work up the courage to say even one word to Lily?

"You need to deal with this," Margret says, and there's an unexpected softness in her tone. "Whatever it is, you need to deal. Because if it ends up on my doorstep, then I'm sorry, but you—"

"It's my girlfriend!" The words blurt out of me like a shot, and my entire body dissolves into cold shivers.

"I'm sorry?" Margret's faint brows shoot up into her gray curls.

"I—" The lie knots my tongue. "That's why they're calling so much. I, uh… I told them I met someone and they want to meet her, but I've been saying no and my mother is not the kind of woman you say no to, so it's creating a lot of pressure to provide details, y'know?"

"A girlfriend?" Margret repeats. "I've never seen you out socializing."

I force a wide smile. "Yeah, uh... I, uh, I met her at the store, and we hit it off, and I, uh... yeah."

"Who?"

"It's a secret," I say quickly. "She's not ready to go public. I am a hotshot doctor, after all."

Margret's eyes narrow, and then her next words send a molten hot bullet right through my gut.

"Well I think since I'm fielding all the calls from your mother, I have a right to know who it is. So invite her."

"Invite her?" I say hoarsely. "To what?"

"The medical charity party, of course. Bring her with you, and I'll evaluate whether she's worth losing my sanity over."

3

LILY

"Emma! Come on, sweetie! We're leaving in ten minutes!"

"Coming!" My daughter's screech carries down the stairs as if she were standing right next to me, and I wince even as a smile creeps over my face.

Dodging questions about her father on the drive home was difficult, especially now I know the other kids are starting to give her a hard time about it. Ever since she was little, I knew this day would come and so I would tell her that her dad was away doing important jobs for people. Sometimes it would be for the princes in her storybooks. Other times it would be to help the Easter Bunny, depending on the time of year.

Those stories worked well on her in the past, but I sense now that she's getting far too smart for me to continue pulling the wool over her eyes. So instead, I deflected and diverted her attention to dinner with her grandparents.

That was enough to distract her, at least for now.

In the kitchen, I lift several spoonsful of pasta into two Tupperware containers. My parents are never short on meals since they run the Fir Tree Inn with a cook who serves lunch and dinner, but there's something nice about bringing them a home-cooked meal.

Above me, Emma's footsteps stomp around, then she charges down the stairs and slides into the kitchen with a wide grin on her face.

"Oh, my God." I snort softly. "Emma, is that really the right thing to wear to go and see Grandma and Grandpa?"

She stands before me with her hands in the air, her body tucked into blue dungarees and a pink tutu visible just underneath. The puff skirt's netting sticks out at her sides through the gaps in the dungarees, and she's placed a tiara on her head.

"Well, Grandpa always likes the tutu, but if I wear these" —Emma pats her dungaree pocket— "I can help Grandma in the garage."

"Ahh, you are a girl of many talents." I chuckle, motioning her forward. "Are you comfortable?"

"Mmhmm!" Emma darts forward and climbs up onto the stool next to me, then she breathes deeply. "Pasta!"

"Yes. You want to try some? Make sure it's good enough?"

Emma nods and her face turns very serious. "We can't bring them a bad dinner."

"No, we certainly can't." Passing her a fork, I slide the empty pot toward her, where a couple of pasta spirals still sit at the bottom, covered in spicy tomato sauce. She digs in immediately, smacking her lips together, and my heart warms.

No matter how my day is or how stressful work ends up being, there's something so heartwarming about coming home to Emma. She eats the spirals and then nods, mimicking Grandma in the way she taps her finger against her chin.

"I think it's just right," Emma declares. She hands the fork back to me and slides off the stool. "Oh, no! I forgot my boots!" With that, she sprints right out of the kitchen and runs all the way up the stairs.

"Five minutes!" I call with a laugh.

Dungarees and a tutu are certainly a choice, but it's just like her to try and look her best for everyone. She's grown up around me busy in the bakery, Grandma busy in the garage attached to the inn, and Grandpa busy with all the inner workings of the Fir Tree Inn. Three different worlds combined in one family.

As I busy about sealing the Tupperware and cleaning up the pot, my phone rings. I answer it with an awkward press of my nose. "Hello?"

"Lily!" Amelia, my best friend, bursts onto the screen with a glass of something pink and fizzy in her hand. "Oh, dear, I was calling to ask if you wanted to come over, but you look busy!"

"Yeah, sorry. I'm taking Emma to the inn. Dinner with the parents tonight." I scrub quickly at the pot, keeping an ear on Emma's noisy footsteps up above. "Thanks, by the way."

"Ooh, what for?"

"For teaching Emma to walk confidently. She's been stomping about ever since I picked her up."

Amelia bursts out laughing and rocks away from the phone. "Oh, love, I'm sorry. I tried to tell her it was about walking tall and stuff, but I think she took me literally."

"Do I need to be worried?" I glance at the phone. "She told me some kids were picking on her."

"About the dance?" Amelia sobers up quickly. "It's just kids being kids. Nothing serious, but I am keeping an eye on it."

"Kids being kids." I sigh. "Little brats, it sounds like."

"Yeah." Amelia sighs and sips her drink. "Besides, the dance is every year and Emma dances with her grandpa, right? The kids will move on quickly."

"She's asking questions, though." Keeping my voice low, I glance at the door to make sure she's not here yet. "I knew it was coming, but she's asking real questions now. I don't think fairy tale answers will fly this year."

"Aw, love." Amelia sighs. "Is there anything I can do?"

I look at her and shake my head. "No. I suppose this was inevitable. I just don't want those kids to find out and make things worse, y'know? I figured I had at least one more year of stories to tell."

"Kids are too smart for their own good," Amelia remarks. "Although it really does sound like you need a drink. You sure you can't slip away?"

"Nah. Tonight is family time," I reply. "Besides, you look like you're three glasses deep."

Amelia laughs and runs a hand through her short, red hair. "Honestly. Oh, the reason I called, though." She waggles her brows at me. "Did I see you talking to Mark in the hall?"

The memory of his oddly dry palm bursts into my mind, and I shiver slightly. "More like he was quizzing me. I got the distinct impression that he was flirting with me."

"And?" Amelia sing songs a little. "What did you think?"

"Of Mark?"

"Yes, of Mark!"

"I don't know." Setting the towel aside, I stack the containers into my bag. "He seemed alright. Average, I guess."

"Average is a good place to start." Amelia grins.

"Amelia. Did you send him to me?"

Her face melts into picture-perfect innocence. "I may have nudged him your way."

"Amelia!"

"What? I don't want my best friend to be sad and lonely at Christmas, okay? You deserve to have someone take you out and treat you, y'know? And he's like the only decent teacher left at the school."

"If he's so great, why don't you take a crack? Because I am not interested."

"Lily, at least think about it." She leans in close and her adorable face fills the screen. "Please? You can't be alone forever."

"I'm not alone," I reply as Emma's thundering steps descend the stairs. "I have Emma and you and my parents and all my friends."

"None of those people can give you what you really need."

"Which is?" I side-eye Amelia as Emma comes into the kitchen.

"I can't say it in polite company," Amelia grinds out, making me laugh.

"Alright. Emma, say hi and bye to Amelia. We've got to go."

"Hi, bye!" Emma calls, waving her hand at the phone.

"Hi, bye," Amelia calls back with a smile. "Alright, love ya, Lily."

"Love you too."

***

Pulling up to the Fir Tree Inn is a little like coming home. While I didn't strictly grow up here, the majority of my childhood and teen years were spent here helping out. Nestled on the edge of the pine forest that sweeps around the town, the Fir Tree Inn is a home for all travelers and tourists. It's survived all this town's rising and falling economy and housed hundreds during and after severe snow storms. The hall is often used for parties and gatherings, especially at New

Year's, and the inn is as much a fixture of the town as the gigantic marble fir tree statue in the middle of the town with the foundation plaque.

Now, it's as beautiful as ever with colorful Christmas lights twinkling along the eaves and the first dusting of heavy snow clinging to the roofs. Orange light warms the entryway, and I glimpse my father bustling about inside.

"Ready?" I turn to face Emma, who is holding tightly onto the pasta boxes. She nods quickly and puffs out her cheeks.

"If I don't eat soon, I'm gonna die!"

"Uh-huh sweetie. Well, let's get inside before that happens." Affectionately rolling my eyes, I help Emma from the car and we head inside. Immediately, we're greeted by a welcoming warmth and the scent of the peppermint sticks that sit by the check-in desk.

"Grandpa!"

"Munchkin!" My dad comes hurrying from the back office and throws his arms out wide for a hug. "Look at you all dressed up!"

"She dressed up for you *and* Mom," I say with a smile as Emma runs into her grandpa's arms. "And we brought dinner."

"Oh, honey, you didn't have to do that!" My mom appears from the side door, wearing dungarees almost identical to the pair Emma wears while wiping grease from her stained fingers. "You know we have a chef."

"I know, but I like to cook for you both." I kiss her cheek and help Emma set the boxes on the desk. "Besides, by the time I heat this up, you'll both have time to get cleaned up and then no one needs to worry about cooking."

"You do think of everything." My dad chuckles while gently wrestling with Emma. He tickles her, picks her up, and spins her around, which makes my mom surge forward.

"Adam, be careful! Watch your back!"

"My back is fine, Hillary," Dad replies. "You worry too much."

"Well, I'd better not hear you complaining about that stool giving you aches when it's your own actions." Mom chuckles and then inspects the boxes. "Oh, my, this smells amazing! Darling, did you see that the ice rink is open? Maybe we can go this weekend?"

"I'll think about it," I say, trying to draw up my calendar from the depths of my tired mind.

"I helped with dinner!" Emma declares, breathless from laughing. "Tell her, Mom!"

"It's true, she helped." I smile. "Right, you two get cleaned up and I'll go get these heated up, alright?"

A round of agreeable murmurs rises from the group. Walking through the lobby, a familiar sense of comfort washes over me. These wooden walls, rickety chairs, and thick carpet have seen everything from me over the years, from failed tests and graduation to crying over boyfriends and fights with the family. It's really a second home.

As I reach the wooden paneled doors leading further into the inn, I glance over my shoulder. "Emma, do you want garlic bread?"

"Yes, please!"

The door swings open as I walk forward, causing my outstretched hand to miss the handle and instead press against the warm, broad chest of the man coming through from the other side.

"Oh, my, I'm so sorry!" I gasp. A jolt of energy fizzes at my palm, then shoots up my arm like the odd, painful reflex of striking your funny bone, and I snatch my hand away. As I do, the containers in my other hand wobble.

The man catches my wrist with soft, strong fingers. With his other hand, he grasps my opposite arm and pulls me against him so our combined torsos prevent the boxes from toppling over and sending pasta all over the floor.

"Oh, God, I'm sorry!" I gasp, torn between staying in a grasp that feels oddly comforting and darting away before the energy simmering under my skin explodes outward.

I've never felt anything like it in my life.

I glance up at the stranger and lock eyes with the most deeply intense blue eyes I have ever seen. They twinkle from golden skin, and a few brown curls drift down to get in the way as the man steadies the both of us and then smiles. His smile is wide and warm, and then the corners turn down slightly as if noticing something.

Something that clicks with me at the same moment.

I jerk away from him, hugging the containers to my chest. That electric feeling… I felt it once before. And I've seen those blue eyes before. I used to get lost in them daily as time continued on without us.

"You," I gasp, and a tremor whips down my spine, forcing my shoulders to shake. "What are you… how are you… what?"

"Hello, Lily," says James Anderson, the man I was certain I would never see again.

4

JAMES

Lily Thompson.

The woman I came halfway across the country to see and then hid from, unable to take that step for fear of what I would see in her eyes.

Now she stands before me, staring up at me, and suddenly, I'm twenty-five again. The world around us melts away, and nothing exists but us.

Her.

She looks exactly as I remember, as if she just stepped right out of my memories. Her long, black hair tumbles around her shoulders in thick waves, with a cluster of curls sweeping across her forehead. She has the greenest eyes I've ever seen in my life, a deep emerald jade sparkling under two lined, dark brows. Freckles dance across her button nose and round cheeks that quickly flush pink under my gaze.

I know every detail of her face, and seeing it again squeezes all the air out of my lungs. She looks the same and yet, different. Time weighs on her, like it does on everyone after seven years, but I couldn't care less. Life leaves its marks, and each line taunts me with the life I could have had with her.

If I had just been stronger and tossed my familial obligations into the wind at an early age, then maybe I would have been happy. Instead, I'm thirty-two years old, mourning the abrupt death of my father, and chasing after the memory of love.

And then Lily smiles. It's a brilliant, broad smile that lights up her entire face and makes my heart skip a painful beat. Breathing is still impossible. I'm wary of making any movement in case it bursts this little bubble I find myself in.

"James." Lily says my name like it's a sweet secret, and it kickstarts me back to life.

I take a breath, and the familiar floral notes of her perfume fill my lungs as my chest cavity clenches, powerful and painful.

"What…" Lily steps back, cradling the containers in her arms. "I can't believe it." Her eyes dart down me, then back up, and I quickly stand a little straighter, hoping she likes what she sees. "What are you even doing here? I–I don't understand."

"A shock, I know." I smile gently and swallow around my tongue, which suddenly feels too fat for my own mouth. "I, uh…" Clasping my hands together for strength, I choose the most honest route. "Well, right now, I'm living here at the Fir Tree. Likely outstayed my welcome by this point, but I've yet to take the leap and secure real property elsewhere."

"Staying here?" Lily's brows shoot up to her hairline. "But why? Why are you staying *here*?"

I realize at that moment that she doesn't know. It was foolish of me, but late at night, I would entertain the fantasy that somehow, Lily would learn I was here and come waltzing into the medical center demanding to see me.

Foolish, I know.

My fear of reaching out seems to have made me too good at staying hidden.

"I work here."

"Here?" Lily glances around and confusion etches itself across her face.

"Well, not *here*. I'm the new gynecologist down at Evergreen Medical Center."

"Wait." Lily laughs softly. "You're the new hot shot doctor?"

"I don't know if I'd call myself a hot shot." I smile back at her. "But yeah, you could say that."

"I… I had no idea." Lily adjusts the containers in her arms. "I mean, I knew there was a new doctor and everyone's been raving about how good you are, but usually when some arrogant big wig takes up a post at the center, they never last long. They never expect a small town to be so demanding." Then Lily's eyes widen and she quickly shakes her head. "Not that I'm saying you're an arrogant doctor, I just mean that…" The crimson flush on her cheeks deepens. "Y'know, other doctors."

"Ahh, of course." I laugh with her. "Don't worry, I understand. And I can empathize on some level with the arrogant ones. The job posting was very lax on the details about *just* how much help was needed, but I do like a challenge."

"So…" Lily's eyes dart back and forth. "That means you've been here for about three months or so? And I've…" Finally, her eyes lock onto mine, and it's like she's punched me right in the chest. "I've never seen you."

Heat slides up my spine like a snake, and I suddenly grow very aware of my hands and where to put them. In my pocket? On my waist? Should I cross them?

"I've been… *busy*," I reply carefully. "Hence why I'm still living in the motel and not in my own place. Too much work to catch up on and not enough time to go out and explore the town, so I'm not surprised."

"Right…" Lily nods slowly. "Wow. I still can't believe you're actually here. I never thought we'd see each other again. I mean just…" Lily clears her throat softly. "How we left things and your, uhm… your family."

Ah. Yes. My family and their ever-tightening leash.

"Perks of a small town!" declares a cheerful voice. Just like that, the bubble bursts and I remember there are other people in the lobby besides me and Lily.

"Does that count, Dad?" Lily says, turning to the man at the counter.

My stomach tightens. *Dad?* He's her father… It seems so glaringly obvious now that I consider the wooden sign hanging outside declaring that the Fir Tree Inn has been loved for thirty-five years by the Thompsons. Mr. Thompson had insisted I call him Adam from the moment I arrived, and I never thought any more about it.

Small town, indeed.

"Of course it counts." Adam chuckles. "Just because it took three months for the two of you to run into each other doesn't mean it doesn't count. It's the beauty of a small town. Sometimes, you run into the same person every day for six months, and other times, you don't see that person for eight."

"Maybe." Lily laughs and adjusts the containers in her arms once more. "I just…" She glances back at me. "It's so… surreal."

"Why, do I look that different?" I joke, trying to break the static influx of nerves flooding my chest.

"No," Lily says, and it's suddenly like she's talking to me in a way only I can hear. "You look exactly the same."

"I'll take that." I chuckle. "Better to look twenty-five than thirty-two."

Seven years. Has it really been that long? It feels infinitely longer and yet now that I'm here, talking to her, it feels like no time at all.

"Oh, Mr. Anderson!" Hillary, who I now know to be Lily's mother, suddenly pops up from behind the counter. "Just the man I was looking for."

"Oh?" I take a half-step past Lily. "Is everything alright?"

"Yes, yes. Don't you worry yourself. I'm just nearly done with your car. These fancier models always take a little extra loving, y'know? But the part I ordered that I didn't think would arrive until after Christmas actually turned up today, so I'll have you back on the road in no time."

"That's fantastic news," I say. "You've already outdone yourself."

"Well, that's good news." Adam grins. "You'll be able to go just about anywhere now. Will you be heading to visit family for Christmas?"

That thought catches in my mind and I hesitate. "Uh… no, no. Not this year. No traveling for me."

Adam's lips part as if ready to ask another question when a young girl skips out from behind the counter and charges straight toward me. She has a mop of brown hair sweeping across her head and trailing behind her as she runs, and striking blue eyes. Just as she reaches me, I notice the smattering of freckles across her nose. Then she passes me and latches onto Lily's leg.

"Mommy!" she cries. "Hurry up. I'm so hungry I'm about to fade away into nothing!"

Lily begins to laugh, and while carefully balancing the boxes in one hand, reaches down the other to pat her daughter's head. "I'm sorry, baby. I'm on it."

"No family at Christmas?" Hillary pipes up.

Just as I search for some kind of excuse, Lily suddenly shoves one of the containers into my arms. "Help me with this?" she asks.

"Gladly."

We quickly escape the awkward family questions, and I breathe a sigh of relief as we walk through the dining hall. "Thank you."

"Don't mention it. My mom is every bit as small-town as they come, and she feeds on information." Lily chuckles. "She never means anything by it, but it can get pretty awkward quickly."

"I can imagine." She does strike me as a lovely woman, but my family can of worms is firmly closed right now. My thoughts linger on Lily and more importantly, her daughter. I didn't know she had a child, and now suddenly, the woman I ache for has all the makings of a true family.

"So, that was your daughter?"

"Mmm, yes. Emma. She's an adorable rascal." Lily smiles. She leads me into the kitchen and takes the Tupperware container from my hands. "She will also ask you awkward questions, but again, that's just curiosity."

"No harm," I say, and I lean against the metal counter. "You and your husband are very lucky."

"Oh." Lily snorts loudly as she works to remove the lids and decant the meals into a large metal pot. "I'm not married."

"Oh, look at me," I say as a wave of relief crashes down on my shoulders. "Now I'm the one assuming things."

"Honestly, as assumptions go about single mothers, that's probably the gentlest one." Lily uses the back of her wrist to push hair away from her eyes, then she flashes me a smile and turns on the heat. "So, James. Why are you here? Of all the places in the world, why are you in this place?"

You. The answer sits heavy on the tip of my tongue, but I can't say it. To admit it would open myself up to the almost certain rejection coming my way, and I want to enjoy this reunion for a little while longer.

"Well…" Taking a deep breath, I brace both hands against the counter. "My dad died."

Lily abruptly pauses her stirring and looks at me with eyes flooded with sorrow. "Oh, James. I'm so sorry."

Waving one hand, I try to pass it off. If I linger too long, then the crushing grief I'm keeping at bay with stress and a dream will flood forward and smother me. "It's okay. I mean it's not but… y'know."

"How did it happen?"

"Heart attack. It was sudden. One minute, he was here, being the life of the room and carving out a legacy and the next, he was just…"

Skimming my hand along the cool countertop, my mind flashes with memories of getting the call and hearing my mother sob on the phone. Of having to shake countless hands as people I barely knew told me what a great man he was. The funeral was more of a show than anything else. I force the memories away and smile tightly.

"Anyway. I just needed… something different. I needed to not be in that world for a while and I needed to do something that felt right to me, so when I came across the job posting, I took it. And now I'm here."

"Wow." Lily shakes her head. "What are the chances that you would end up in my little town, huh?"

"Probably one in a million." I can't take my eyes off her. When I look at her, the pain and fog in my mind vanishes, and the acidic sorrow in my chest warms to affection instead. Such power she has on me and we are, effectively, strangers.

"One in a trillion." She laughs, stirring. "I'm sorry about your dad. But, coming here… has it helped? Have you found what you're looking for?"

She lifts her head and we lock eyes as I nod slowly. "I think so, yes."

"That's good!" Her smile widens. "It's the little things that help us, isn't it?"

"You could say that. Although I have run into a slight hiccup in terms of surviving here."

"Oh?" Lily sweeps her hair over one shoulder as she collects bowls from a cupboard. "Anything I can help with? Trust me, I know everyone in this place so if someone is giving you trouble, I definitely have some tips."

"It's less the town and more… my family. See, my mother isn't too happy about my ditching my life there and creating one here, so she's blowing up my phone and every phone within my vicinity."

Lily stiffens slightly as she spoons the pasta into four bowls.

"And Margret, my boss, made it clear that she was tired of it and it was beginning to override the work I was doing there, and if I'm not careful, I'll be out on my ear."

As I talk, a spur-of-the-moment idea springs into mind.

"And so I told her the reason my mom has been so stalkerish is because I'm dating someone and she wants to be introduced and I'm not ready for that, so I'm fielding her calls. And then Margret demanded I bring my date to the medical charity party because she feels like she's owed it."

"Makes sense." Lily chuckles and licks her spoon. "So, what's the issue? Your date doesn't want to go?"

"No…" Straightening up, I clasp my hands together. "I don't have a date."

Lily pauses her movements and watches me. "So you lied."

"I lied." I nod. "But I mean, maybe you could help me with that? I know it's kind of crazy, but you're the only person around here that I know, so maybe that's just fate trying to give me a hand, y'know? I don't want to lose this job, so I need Margret on my side and able to dodge the stalker behavior from my mother, and I know she would just love to feel like she's holding onto a juicy secret." It floods out of me in a rush, like I'm sixteen again asking a girl to prom.

"So, would you be interested?"

"Interested?" Lily's cheeks flush once more.

"In being my date? For a night? I mean, being a fake girlfriend doesn't come with that much glamor, and we haven't seen each other in years, but could you take pity on me?"

Lily's gaze is unwavering, and my heart starts to pound like the rapid thump of a drum.

"Please?"

Lily tilts her head as she thinks and then, to my surprise, she nods. "Okay."

5

LILY

"You said *yes*?" Amelia's screech draws the attention of at least six other shoppers. I grab her by the wrist and drag her down the next empty aisle.

"Shush!" I hiss, barely holding back a laugh at Amelia's comically surprised face. "But yeah, I did."

"Why? What were you thinking? Why would you say yes? What will you—Lily, why?"

"I don't know, okay?" Releasing Amelia, my hand returns to the shopping cart and I try to distract myself by scanning the shelves for what's left on my list. Emma's currently with my parents, which gives me a few hours to grab necessities that were missing from my weekly delivery.

"Are you sure?" Amelia falls into step beside me, popping a few grapes into her mouth that she snagged from the pack in my cart. "I mean, the man broke your heart, Lily. He abandoned you and Emma, and then the first time you see him, you agree to be his girlfriend?"

"Fake girlfriend," I correct quickly. "And I don't know. Seeing him again was like…" Sighing, I shrug my shoulders. Butterflies entered my stomach the moment I bumped into him yesterday, and that feeling has not gone away. "It was like I was twenty-one again. He looks exactly the same, and I mean like *exactly* the same. He's still so hot, and then he was sad, okay? He was standing there talking about his dad dying and not knowing anyone in town, and maybe losing his job because of his mother, and I just… I felt really, really bad for him."

"The same mother he used to dump you?" Amelia snorts. "Maybe he should lose his job. That would be some good Karma."

"I don't know. He just looked so sad. It was like I could suddenly see how he was holding himself together with tape and the seams were cracking, and I just saw a way I could help him, y'know?"

"You are a bleeding heart," Amelia sighs, then she loops her arm around my shoulders and pulls me close. "But I wouldn't have you any other way."

"Thanks." I laugh softly. We pause so I can gather several bags of flour, and then we carry on.

"So, what are you going to do?" Amelia steals another few grapes from the pouch. "Hang on his arm, look pretty, and let the entire town think you're dating the hot new doctor?"

"I guess? It's better than their thinking I'm some old spinster or trying to set me up with their weird friends."

"You mean Mark?" Amelia snorts. "I'm sorry. I really thought you guys would hit it off."

"I appreciate your looking out for me. I think with James I just need to attend the party. It's the charity auction, I think?" We wheel around to the next aisle, and I smile politely as we pass some people. "Just enough for Margret to think she's got a scoop on some gossip, and then he'll have one less thing to worry about. I mean, his dad died. And he worshiped that guy. If it wasn't for him and those seminars across the country, we never would have met, and while all of that ended in heartbreak, I got Emma. So maybe it's the least I can do."

"Your heart is too big to share a piece with someone who already hurt you," Amelia says, and her shoulder rubs against mine. "But nah, I get it. Do you think you will tell him, then? About Emma?"

"God, no." There's no way in hell I am telling him the truth. "He might look the same, but we're not the same people we were. I'm not risking damaging Emma's life just because he's randomly shown up. He didn't want to know then, so he doesn't get to know now."

"That's my girl." Another shoulder rub, and Amelia darts away toward the confectionaries.

In her absence, my mind runs in circles. James's being here is like something out of a dream and I can't get his stupid, handsome face out of my mind. I spent all last night tossing and turning as I replayed our last days together and how bumping into him yesterday felt painfully natural. It was like no time had passed and we were the same two love-struck people.

And now I was to be his date. A good idea at the time. He just looked so sad and forlorn behind that smile of his that it was all I could do to stop myself from hugging him. Amelia's right. I am a bleeding heart.

"Okay, I am all set." Amelia returns with a box of brownies and adds them to the cart. "Oh, actually. Would it be terrible for me to ask you to bake something for me?"

"I'd be offended if you didn't."

"I want something sweet for my class for the end of term, and I was thinking of those Christmas shortbread cookies you made last year?" Amelia turns to me with large puppy-dog eyes. "Could you whip me up a batch for my kids this year? I'll pay you, I promise."

"And here I thought you were going to take advantage of my bleeding heart." I laugh. "Sure. Just let me know how many you need and when."

* * *

"Mooooom!" Emma's voice carries through the bakery like birdsong, only scratchier, and I laugh despite being elbow deep in dough.

"I'm in the back, sweetie!"

Emma comes sprinting through, followed a few seconds later by my mom.

"Hi, darling." Mom presses a kiss to my cheek and then scoffs softly. "Goodness, Lily, you've got flour all over you."

I send her a sidelong glance as Emma attaches to my leg. "Would you use the same tone if I were covered in motor oil?"

"In a bakery?" Mom teases. "Absolutely."

Rolling my eyes, I crouch down the best I can and kiss Emma's head. "Hi, baby. How was Grandma's?"

"It was so good!" Emma bounces up and down excitedly. "She let me drive the car!"

"What?" I jerk back upright as my heart rate rapidly increases. "What?"

"No, no, no!" Mom laughs and grabs Emma, pulling her away from me and tickling her. "I just had her sit in the driver's seat and test pedals for me while I was working on something. I promise, no driving took place."

"Oh, thank God," I breathe out.

"You rascal, I told you if we told your mom it would give her a heart attack!" Mom tickles Emma mercilessly, and she squeals and giggles for a few minutes until she's released.

"I did not need to envision my six-year-old behind the wheel of a car," I groan, although the sudden spike of anxiety renews my forceful kneading of the dough in my hands.

"I was driving when I was six," Mom says. "Of course, things were different back then."

"Did road safety even exist when you were a kid?" I tease, earning myself a gentle smack on my arm.

"Cheeky. I'm not that old!" Mom kisses Emma's head and ruffles her hair. "Anyway, I'd better get back. This one has been running around all day, and we had dinner, so you don't need to worry about that."

"Thank you, I appreciate it."

"Of course!" Mom kisses my cheek. "Bye, baby."

"Bye, Mom."

"And I'll see you tomorrow, munchkin."

"Bye, Grandma!"

Emma busies herself, dragging her stool across the bakery kitchen and setting it beside me, then she climbs up and sighs deeply, as if she's just back from a nine-hour shift.

"Whatcha making?"

"It's a secret," I say, smiling affectionately down at her. "I can't tell you."

"Why not?" Emma pouts up at me and her eyes become saucers.

"Because it's a secret that involves you!" With Amelia being Emma's teacher, Emma becomes one of the students Amelia wants to surprise with these treats and I'm not going to ruin that for her.

"Me?" Emma gasps and then pokes her little fingers at some stray dough on the counter. "A secret," she whispers. Her head darts up to look at me. "Are you sure you can't tell me?"

"I'm sure," I whisper in reply. "But it will be worth it, I promise."

As Emma whispers her agreement, the bakery phone lights up with a call and a soft song plays out. Years ago, I'd picked up the phone at a charity shop because it was shaped like bread and I got a kick out of it. Nothing prepared me for the first time I got a call, though, and instead of a ringing bell sound, the phone sang to me in French.

To this day, I still don't know the song.

"I'll get it!"

Emma's about to slide off her stool when I gently catch her wrist. "No, sweetie. You stay here, okay? In fact, while I'm on the phone, can you knead the dough for me? Just like I've shown you before."

"Sure!" Emma lights up at the prospect and immediately shoves her hands into the sticky dough as I retract my fingers. She falls into the rhythm easily, and I keep one eye on her as I hurriedly wipe my hands and answer the phone.

"Hello? You've reached *Sweet Noel.*"

"Lily!" Margret's rough, scratchy tones crawl over the line. "I was beginning to think you would never pick up!"

"Well," I say with a glance at the clock, "it is after nine and I'm usually home by now."

"Yes, yes, I did try your home phone and your cell, but no answer," Margret replies.

As she talks, I pat my pockets and locate my mobile only to find the screen completely dark.

"I'm sorry, Margret, I think I forgot to charge it again. Time gets away from me when I'm baking."

"You should be more careful," Margret says. "It's not safe to be out and about without your phone charged."

"I know, I know," I assure her quickly. It's the same spiel she's given me since I was a teenager, although it increased in frequency after Emma was born. I know she means well, but I have a terrible time remembering to charge it.

"Well, since you're still working, I was hoping to speak to you about something."

"Of course!" My heart skips a beat while my stomach churns. Did James tell her that I'm his date? Am I about to get questioned about every detail of my life?

"About the cake?"

My mind screeches to a halt. "I'm sorry, the cake?"

"Did Taylor not get in touch with you last week?" Margret rasps. "About the cake for the charity auction?"

From the depths of my overactive mind surges the information on the cake I was hired to make, and a hot flush of foolishness warms the back of my neck.

"Oh, my God, Margret. You're right, don't worry. Taylor definitely did call about a cake last week, and I have all the details. It just completely slipped my mind!"

"You had me worried there, dear." Margret chuckles. "The auction was your idea, after all."

"I know, I know. I just have a lot of spinning plates right now." Mainly, the realization that James's *Medical Party* and the *Charity Auction* are one and the same. Somehow, I didn't put two and two together when he was asking me to be his date, but it seems so obvious now.

"It's a good thing you are doing," Margret continues. "I've always been in support of a free clinic, especially these days. And now that we have this fancy new doctor, I bet he'd be willing to donate a few hours to the clinic too."

"You think?" I shift the phone against my ear while keeping one eye on Emma. "I mean, a lot of what we have to auction has been gifted by the people, and there's a few art pieces from the gallery. If you could get Ja— that new doctor to donate some hours, I bet that would ease some of the costs of getting this place up and running?"

"I'll talk to him," Margret assures me. "Although after one mouthful of one of your cakes, I'm sure he'll say yes to anything you ask him!"

I laugh off the compliment, smoothing one hand down my apron. The clinic itself does wonders, but after Emma's birth and a few health struggles she had in her early years, I racked up medical bills that were painful to pay off. I was lucky, though, that I was even able to, and the thought of a free clinic was something I raised often at the Town Hall.

This year they finally said yes, if I can raise enough money to get it off the ground.

"Okay, so Margret, just to check. Taylor commissioned me for a four-tier cake made from vanilla, lemon, chocolate, and toffee, with a cream cheese frosting and marzipan town trademarks, correct?" I ask while reeling off the order details scrawled on a blue sticky note next to the till.

"That's the one!"

"Amazing. So, most of the decorating work is done and ready. The cake just needs to be baked and assembled, and then we can freeze it until the party."

"Is there any chance we can freeze it here?" Margret asks. "I keep thinking about the snow storms and if it's as bad as last year, then I don't want the cake to be stuck there with all the snow."

"Good point. Tell you what, I can build the four tiers here, then send them to you for storage. Then, on the night, I can assemble in-house, and that way, we don't miss out on the star of the show!"

"Excellent," Margret croaks. "I'll send the new guy over to pick it up when it's all ready. Thanks!"

She hangs up before I can say much else, but as I hang up the phone, my twisting gut suddenly tightens.

The new guy.

She's going to send James!

Despite meeting him yesterday and agreeing to be his fake date, the prospect of his coming here to *my* bakery makes my stomach somersault.

Why does that make me so incredibly nervous?

6

JAMES

"It's just coffee but instead of caramel, you use the orange syrup, and with two pumps it's honestly *amazing*." Taylor stares at me over the edge of her cup. "Don't knock it until you try it."

With only a plain old coffee for myself, I smile at Taylor and shake my head. "I'm good with regular caffeine, thanks, but I'll try and remember you like yours weird."

"It's not weird!" Taylor yelps softly. "You're just uncultured in the ways of coffee."

"You know, you might be right. I've spent my life in cities with a Starbucks on every corner."

"Ew," Taylor groans. "We need to get you into a coffee correction course."

"Pencil that in for me." I laugh, waving goodbye to her. Just as I head back to my office, I run into Margret who smiles at me slyly and immediately sets my nerves on edge.

"Yes?"

"So, are you going to give me a hint as to who you are dating?"

"Why does it matter?"

"My life is helping others." Margret scoffs. "The least you can do is fuel me with the exciting twists and turns in your own life."

"You just want the gossip so you can smile like that to everyone in town so they know you have a secret," I say, stopping at my door with one hand on the handle. "So I'm not telling you."

"Not even a tiny hint?"

"Okay, I'll give you one."

It's comical the way Margret's face lights up with hope.

"She'll be at the charity party."

Margret's face falls immediately, and she curses me under her breath as I laugh myself into my office and kick the door closed. By the time I reach my desk after a few sips of coffee, I realize Taylor might be right. The coffee here is amazing. I don't think I can ever go back to what they serve in the city.

Not that I have plans to ever head back there.

As if she could read my thoughts, my cell blares into life, and my mother's number splashes across the screen. Her calls are becoming impossible to dodge. I can't do anything on my phone without risking hitting the answer call button while trying to access an app, but if I block her, I know she'll go as far as to report me missing to the police.

With no patients lined up, I take a chance and answer.

"Hello?"

"James! Oh, my goodness!" My mother's powdery tones make my chest tighten suddenly, and my heart rate picks up.

"What is it?"

"Is that any way to greet your mother? I haven't spoken to you in weeks and yet you speak to me as if I'm some cold caller!"

"That's not—"

"Whatever did I do to earn such an ungrateful son? When I need you the most, you swan off across the country and stop taking calls. Bernice and I are worried sick about you in case something happens. When your own fiancée can't get in touch with you, it makes everyone fear something is wrong!"

Sagging forward onto my desk, I press my fingers against the bridge of my nose. "Mom."

"And to think, after everything I have done for you, when I need you the most, you run away. No warning. Just up in the night and disappearing. Do you have any idea what that's done for my nerves? You need to make this right, understand? You need to come home."

She pauses for a breath, finally, and I can speak. "Mom. You know Bernice is not my fiancée anymore. She hasn't been for six months."

"Oh, nonsense. It's just a hiccup that will work itself out. I know for a fact that she will forgive you when you come back."

"I'm not coming back. And even if I did, just because you want something to work out doesn't mean it will. Don't you see? Didn't Dad's death teach you anything? You can't plan every single detail of my life, okay? Things change. Disasters happen."

"Your father would be *ashamed* to hear you say such things! You should be here with your family, grieving around loved ones, not away in some backwater town doing God knows what. Now, I gave you space and time, but enough of this foolishness, James. You need to come home now."

"No."

"What?" Her gasp is so loud I have to jerk the phone away from my ear.

"I said no. I've moved on. Changed things. I'm trying to be happy, Mom. I wasn't happy there. I hated my job. Bernice and I didn't like each other, never mind love. I… I'm sorry, but I can't live to make you happy anymore. I need to make *me* happy."

"James, are you listening to yourself? Of course Bernice loves you, what a silly thing to say! If you would just come back and speak to her—"

"No."

"I'm not well, James."

There it is. When her demands and orders don't work, Mom never fails to pull out the guilt trip.

"You need to come home."

"No, Mom. I'm not. And I know you're not well, but I can't help you with that."

"You sullen boy, how can you say something so cruel to your own mother?"

"Mom, it's not—"

"No, no, you need to come home right now and apologize. To me. To everyone. How damn selfish can you be?"

"I'm hanging up now."

"Don't you dare!"

"Bye, Mom. Stop calling me."

I don't hear her last words as I lower the phone and end the call, but I can guess what they are. My next breath is short as the tightness in my chest threatens to overwhelm me. Maybe Dad would be ashamed of me, but I hope he would see the value in my efforts to make myself happy.

To get back what I lost.

Lowering my head, it rests in my palm as I focus on my breathing. I don't move until the tightness in my chest finally passes and my breathing is a touch easier.

"James?" Margret knocks on the door and pokes her head around. "You got some time?"

"Yes." I nod quickly, eager for a distraction. "You got a patient for me?"

"One better. I need you to pop over to Sweet Noel and take some pictures of the cake she's making for the party so we can start advertising."

* * *

Sweet Noel. The bakery I've passed countless times but never had the guts to enter. Learning that Lily was making a cake for the charity event was a surprise since she never mentioned it when I invited her to be my fake date. Then again, we didn't do much talking after her parents entered the kitchen eager to eat.

The bakery is tucked on the corner of the square with golden lights woven around the wooden sign. Fake snowflakes and frosting dot the windows around countless gorgeous cupcakes, muffins, and colorful sponges I couldn't even name.

I take a deep breath and push open the door. Soft Christmas music dances through the air, weaving between the mouthwatering scents of bakery and sugar. Cinnamon tickles my nose, alongside peppermint and the cozy warmth of rising cakes.

I'm greeted with a glass counter, behind which sit some of the more intricate cakes and tarts, all with their own handwritten cards telling customers what they are. Tinsel clings to the top of the counters, and a few glittering Santas dangle down from the ceiling.

Christmas is a few weeks away, and this is the first time I've felt remotely festive.

Approaching the counter, I tap the silver bell. "Hello?"

"Two seconds!" comes Lily's voice from the other side of a wooden door.

I'm happy to wait but just as I settle against the counter, Lily bustles through the door. Her dark hair is scooped up on top of her head. Flour dots her cheeks and covers her frilly teddy bear apron, and there are colorful streaks on her fingers that I presume to be icing.

Her smile wavers slightly when we lock eyes. "James?"

"Hi." I awkwardly wave one hand.

"Is everything okay? What are you doing here?"

I laugh softly. "Would it be so strange of me to want to buy a cake?"

Lily smooths her hands down her apron, streaking the colors. "No, sorry. I just didn't expect to see you."

"Margret asked me to come."

Lily's eyes widen. "What? The cake isn't ready!"

"No, no, she just wants me to take pictures so she can start teasing it online."

"Oh." Lily puffs out her rosy cheeks and places one hand against her chest. "You scared me for a second. Do you want to buy something as well?"

"I would but I didn't come prepared," I joke. "Next time, though."

Lily's smile is a little shy, then she waves a hand at me. "Okay, come through the back. The cake's in storage, but you can get your pictures."

Lily leads me to the back of the bakery where countless half-finished cakes and desserts line trays and trolleys. It's amazing to see, especially knowing she does all this herself. No wonder she's award-winning.

"It smells amazing back here," I say, carefully avoiding drops of flour on the floor.

"Doesn't it?" Lily beams at me. "I'm in the middle of a commission for a hundred cupcakes for some function in the city, and they changed from lemon to marble at the last minute, so things are a bit hectic."

"Ahh. I did see that you have quite the website presence. All those glowing reviews—it's really impressive."

"Thanks." Lily smiles wider and her rosy cheeks shine. "It's hard but it's worth it. Anyway, the cake's in here. Take what pictures you need."

Lily opens up a gigantic freezer and ushers me inside. On a metal table in the middle sit four thick cakes, and their decorations take my breath away. Each layer is themed after parts of the town, and it's like looking at a detailed miniature reconstruction. From the forest and the inn to the town square, the Christmas fair, and even the gigantic fallen tree that signals the turn into town. It's all here in extreme detail.

"Holy shit. Lily, this is… this is amazing. You did all this?"

Lily's fingers twist together as she nods. "Yep."

"It's incredible. Your talent is just… simply mind-blowing."

Her cheeks darken further. "You're going the right way to a free cupcake." She chuckles.

Lily leaves me to it, and I take as many pictures as I can, from all angles, so Margret can pick her favorites. I get as close as I dare, wary of disturbing Lily's masterpiece. While the chill of the freezer was alarming at first, it quickly became comfortable, but it's nice to walk back out into the heat of the bakery. The tray of blank cupcakes I passed before is now filled with sparkling decorated ones, and I laugh softly.

"You're fast."

Lily shrugs at her work station. "All it takes is practice."

"Lily?"

"Hmm? You get what you need?" She sets down her piping bag and turns to face me.

"Let me take you to dinner."

Lily's smile vanishes. "James. I agreed to be your pretend girlfriend and your fake date to the charity event because I know Margret and I don't want you to lose your job. But that's it. There doesn't have to be anything else."

"I know, I know. Look." I hesitantly step forward. "I know we have… history."

Lily's lips press in a firm line.

"But you're the only person I know here. I've been here a few months but I haven't really reached out to anyone, and seeing a familiar face, it's amazing. And I want to thank you for being my fake date, so please, let me take you to dinner. As friends. It can be a chance for us to get to know each other so we can sell this to Margret. She gives me the impression that she'll be able to sniff us out really fast."

Lily looks thoughtful for a moment, then her shoulders drop and she nods. "Fair point, actually. Okay. You can take me to dinner. As friends."

I hold up my hands. "Strictly amicable. Are you free tomorrow night?"

Lily glances at the dinosaur calendar on the wall and nods. "Yes, actually. Emma has a sleepover, so I'll be free."

"Excellent!" Those giddy butterflies once again sweep through my gut. "I'll pick you up tomorrow, then."

Lily finally smiles again, and its warmth soothes my churning stomach. "Tomorrow, then."

She does grant me a free cupcake, and I carry it out with me, only to almost lose it when a man shoves open the door to the bakery and nearly collides with me.

"Sorry, pal!" He clasps my shoulder, and I catch a whiff of chalk as we pass by one another. He continues inside as I step out into the frosty afternoon air, but when I glance back inside, my heart freezes.

The strange man is embracing Lily tightly, and all the warmth she left me with vanishes.

Who the hell is that guy?

Could he be... Emma's father?

7

LILY

"Alright, sweetie, you be good for Grandma, okay?" Kneeling down, I adjust the buttons on Emma's blouse and cup her cheeks. "I know how much you enjoy a sleepover, but you still have to be on your best behavior, okay?"

"Okay, Mommy!" Emma grins happily at me. "We're gonna play storekeeper!"

"Oh, really?" Laughing softly, I ruffle her curls and stand as my dad comes out from the back of the inn.

"Lily! And Emma, look at you. Are you ready for your sleepover?"

"Yes, Grandpa!" Emma beams up at him, then she waves at me with a tiny fist and scurries off behind the counter. I hear my mom's excited exclamation a moment later.

"Can you keep an eye on her?" I ask Dad while I smooth out the rumples in my T-shirt. "I'm a little worried about her."

"Worried how?" Mom pokes her head through the door like a magpie spotting something shiny. "What's wrong?"

"Emma's just having a little rough patch with some kids at school, so I just want you to keep an eye on her and make sure she's okay, that's all," I explain. "It's nothing too serious yet."

"We will," Dad assures me with a comforting squeeze of my arm. "You don't have to worry. You have a night to yourself. Go and have fun."

"It's about time you got back out into the dating world," Mom agrees as she busies herself, shuffling papers at the front desk. "It's not good to be alone this long."

"One, there's nothing wrong with being alone. And I'm not alone. I have family and friends. And two, it's not a date. It's just dinner with a friend who I am pretending to date to help him out of a tough situation. It's not real."

"Sure." Dad chuckles. "And I was born yesterday." He chuckles to himself and heads through the door to the back of the inn to find Emma.

"You don't need to pretend with us," Mom says, moving around the desk to take my hand. "You're a grown-up. You make your own choices, but you don't need to hide a date from us."

I should try to persuade her that it's really not a date, but that would take longer than I have time for. Instead, I thank her for taking care of Emma for the night and promise to pick her up in the morning. Then, I drive home while my mind races on what on earth to wear.

"What about that little black dress?" Amelia asks me half an hour later on the phone, after I spent twenty minutes tearing apart my closet and called her in desperation.

"It doesn't fit," I whine softly. "That dress is from before I had Emma, and my body then was very different from my body now."

"You're still gorgeous," Amelia says gently.

"I never said I wasn't," I point out. "I just have a few more squishy bits that didn't exist when I bought that dress."

"Hold up the phone. Show me what else you've got in there."

I do as she asks and hold the phone with one hand while dragging a brush through my hair with the other. "I don't even know why I'm so nervous. It's not a real date."

"Sure, but it's in public and that's the lie you're trying to spin," Amelia counters. "That's sure to drag up all sorts of feelings, considering who he is."

"There are no feelings," I murmur.

"Don't think you can lie to me just because I can't see your face right now." I can hear Amelia sucking on her teeth and bite back a smile. "What's that at the back? It looks red but black at the same time?"

"Uhm." Following her instructions, I hunt out a knee-length, strapless dress that's deep red with a love heart neckline. It's covered in sheer black fabric that deepens the red whenever the material ruffles.

"Ooh," Amelia breathes. "That's gorgeous!"

"Also from my pre-Emma days."

"So? It totally looks like it would fit. I mean, you might knock your teeth out with your tits if you run down some stairs, but who cares?"

Snorting with laughter, I set the phone down on the dresser and slide the dress from the hanger. "I'm telling you. I have too many squishy bits."

"Try it," Amelia insists.

With nothing to lose, I do just that. To my immense surprise, the dress slips on easily and the side zip closes like a glove just under my armpit. The dress is snug and Amelia was right. It does push my boobs up slightly, but that only makes the dress look more outstanding.

"Hot mama!" Amelia cheers. "See, I knew it as soon as I saw it. Trust me. Show up in that and he'll regret fielding all those calls seven years ago."

"I'm not trying to make him regret that," I say, plucking at the black sheet netting. "I'm just trying to help him out because—"

"Because you're a softie," Amelia finishes for me. "I know. But this is kind of a sexy revenge dress if I ever saw one. Ooh, add some black pumps and red lippy, and you are *stunning*!"

It takes me a little longer to apply makeup. It's not part of my everyday routine since I learned pretty quickly that the heat of the bakery makes me sweat off anything I have on my face, and no one wants running foundation dripping over their cupcakes. It's satisfying to go all out, though, and paint my face up to help make myself feel beautiful.

"Damn," Amelia whines as I set the last eyelash into place. "How about you ditch James and come out with me instead?"

"Ha!" A final swipe of balm across my red lips and I'm ready. Standing back from the mirror, I pluck at the dress again and take a deep breath. "You think I look good?"

"Lily, you look amazing," Amelia promises me. "Go make him regret ever walking away from you."

——

It was never my goal to make James Anderson regret turning his back on me all those years ago, but it lingers in my mind as I walk up to his table and watch his face melt into a mix of shock and awe. He stands, smoothing one hand down his shirt, and then he darts around the table to pull my chair out for me.

"Lily, my God, you look amazing," he says, easing me into my seat.

"Thank you." I smile up at him, fighting how the compliment blooms in my chest. "We have to make this believable, right? In case anyone sees?"

"Right. Of course." James smiles at me, but the way his eyes constantly dart down me shows he's nervous. He wants to look at me but he's trying to be polite.

I like the tingly feeling it gives me. "You look nice too," I say once he's seated and comfortable.

"Thanks." James laughs softly. "Believe it or not, I don't own much else other than work stuff and a few comfy clothes."

"You didn't pack before coming here?"

"Not really. It was so… spur of the moment that I just bought what I needed along the way."

Of course he did. Money has never been an object for James. I can't imagine having that kind of relaxed outlook on life, but given the work he does as a doctor, maybe it's okay.

"That's crazy." I chuckle. "I need a whole collection whenever I want to travel. For me and Emma. Basically, packing up the entire house because you never know what you might need."

"I can imagine."

James's smile is warm and easy. As we make small talk, his nervous eye-darting calms and soon, he's holding my gaze as easily as he did all those years ago. It's almost too easy to forget how much time has passed since then. We order drinks and food, and as we eat, the conversation turns to the one work thing we have in common.

"Margret told me that you're actually the one behind the entire charity auction party, is that right?" James asks after a mouthful of red wine.

"Yes." I nod, spearing some steak onto my fork. "Crazy, right? Why does a baker care about a medical clinic?"

"Not that crazy," James replies. "I've only been here a short while, but one thing I've noticed about this town is that everyone is involved in everything. There are no set roles or expectations to stay in the lane like there are in the city. You all branch out to help one another."

"Yeah," I say between bites. "I suppose we do. I had this idea that uhm, well, medical bills are painful for anyone. And when Emma was born, she was sick for a while, so those bills piled up."

"Oh, God." James lowers his fork. "I'm so sorry."

I wave one hand and sip my wine. "Don't be. It's just a fact of life, right? You get sick, say goodbye to all your money. Anyway, I was extremely lucky in that my parents helped me with those bills, but it still scraped all of us dry. If not for the inn being so successful, I might have feared for them. But it got me thinking, y'know? Around here, money is tight. Medical treatment is scarce unless you want to pack up to the city, which is an eye-watering expense in itself."

James nods along while he eats, and his eyes never leave mine.

"A free clinic would be able to take the weight off, in some cases. I think about how many serious illnesses can be prevented if they're caught quickly enough, and then not only is the cost down, but people get to live their lives, y'know?"

"It's admirable," James says, and when he smiles, my stomach clenches tightly. Butterflies dance through me, and warmth sweeps up my spine. I'm glad this dress is strapless because with any more layers, I would be sweating up a storm.

"You think so?"

"Of course." His voice is low, and each time I glance up, he's watching me intently. "You can imagine that where I come from, there's not much room for that kind of appreciation for others. For one thing, my mother plans out almost every detail of her life—and mine. A passion project like that is a dream. And I think it's admirable that you're taking time to better things for others."

It's impossible to keep the smile from my face as my cheeks flush warm. "It just feels like a nice thing to do."

"It is. Margret told me that you plan to auction off the tiers of your cake to help raise money, and that lots of other people around town are donating items and pieces to help. Then she asked me if I would be willing to donate hours."

My heart jumps, and I watch him closely. "Will you?"

"I'd be honored." His smile widens, and my heart skips another beat. "Although it's slightly selfish, perhaps, of me to be so willing simply so I can integrate into town a little easier."

"I don't know," I murmur. "I think you're doing a good job."

"Really?" James toys with his glass, sliding his fingers around the rim as we lock eyes.

"Yes," I say, and my mouth is oddly dry. "Everyone's been talking about the hot shot doctor."

"Almost as much as I hear about the award-winning baker," James replies just as swiftly.

My cheeks burn. "That's not really anything."

"Don't downplay your achievements. Doctor. Baker. Mechanic. It doesn't matter. Talent and skill are recognized, regardless. And I know talent when I see it. I always thought you had an intricate eye for detail."

"Really?" I can't look away. His eyes hold me captive, and I'm so completely willing. Under the table, our legs cross, and there's a moment when shin catches against shin. A jolt passes through me, the shock at the contact and yet something more. A familiar ache.

How we used to lie in bed watching the sun come up with our legs tangled together. Things are so different now.

"Definitely." James speaks slowly, like the word is a delicacy, and he doesn't look away. I have to. I'm afraid if I stare too long, I'll fall into his eyes with no way out. But when I glance back up, he's still watching me with such soft intent that I melt.

"It's just practice."

"Practice hones skill, but it doesn't create natural talent," James says. "From the moment I saw you, I knew you had something special about you. This incredible warmth is visible in everything you do."

He speaks like there are no years between us. I'm acutely aware of every movement he makes and how easy it would be to reach across the table and take his hand. I want to feel his touch against my skin and see if it still gives me the same electric shivers it used to.

"You're just saying that because I gave you a free cupcake." I glance away.

Has the air around here gotten thicker? Why is it so hot?

James laughs. "You could solve so much with a free cupcake."

"Everyone loves a good bit of baking."

We talk late into the night, discussing simple things like our day to day lives and then a little bit about the old days. It's hard not to reminisce, and while I was certain if I ever saw James again, I would demand to know why he abandoned me, the question never came up.

I'm having too much fun, and as the restaurant closes and James pays our bill, it hits me how easily this 'fake dating' situation could run away with itself.

I need to be careful.

"I had a fantastic time tonight," James says as we stand on the sidewalk with the bitter cold winter air weaving around us. I'm distantly aware of how cold it is but somehow, it doesn't reach the forefront of my mind.

"Me too." I smile warmly up at him. "We should be well on our way to fooling Margret."

"Ahh, yes," James chuckles. "Margret."

He steps closer, and the world melts away. James has always been incredibly handsome, and now, with the restaurant's twinkling lights as a backdrop and snow dancing in the air, he looks positively mouth-watering.

Alcohol warms my veins, and I feel at peace after a good meal. My skin flushes hot the longer he stares at me without saying a word, then his lips part.

"Taxi for Thompson?" A voice to my left cuts through everything, and I'm quickly jerked back to reality.

"That's me." I smile at the driver who's pulled up alongside us, then glance back at James. "This was nice. Thank you. Goodnight."

"Goodnight, Lily."

The soft way he says my name sticks with me as I slide into the taxi and begin the drive home. Seven years ago, if he'd said my name like that, I would have dragged him into the taxi with me, and his clothes would be on the floor by the time we got home.

I tell myself I have to be strong.

And yet, as I close my eyes and settle into the drive home, all I can think about is how badly I wanted to kiss him.

8

JAMES

Knowing I shouldn't put any stock into how successful dinner was with Lily and actually preventing myself from doing so are two different things.

Ever since dinner, I've been unable to get her out of my head way more than normal. The image of her in that stunning red dress is on constant rotation in my mind, as is how good it felt to sit and talk with her again. Like always, she made me feel seen. Like I was the most important person in her entire world just for a few hours, and it was like no time at all had passed.

I kept bracing myself for her to ask why I had left and why I had gone back with my father, but the question never came. That was probably a good thing, as I think the night would have taken a different turn had our conversation gone that route.

Luckily, everything stayed fun and dare I say, romantic. My feelings for Lily are still as strong as ever, though I was unclear on exactly how she was feeling. Her smiles felt like little secrets that I needed to earn.

Our 'date' had gone down well at work too, since the very next day I turned up to work, Margret was all over the news. She kept telling me over and over again how wonderful Lily is and how I'd made an excellent choice. It also made her very understanding about fielding calls from my mother as, in her words, Lily is far too gentle to be subjected to an overbearing mother until she's ready. People in this town really have a lot of respect for Lily, and it shows.

So, my job is no longer on the line, and I am no longer seen as someone bringing in trouble. Instead, Margret and Taylor are happy to help me dodge my overbearing mother, and after a quick Google search, Taylor was able to forward the call back to herself. That loop gave us a few days of peace as my mother tried to work out how she kept calling herself.

One thing I didn't count on was how quickly the news would spread around town. When I was out shopping for groceries, people I had never seen before came up to talk to me like we were old friends, and they all had something in common.

They all praise me and congratulate me on dating Lily. She's a sweetheart, a great catch, deserving of love and more. The more I go about my day, the more I learn just how loved she is in town. Deirdre from the bookstore stopped me in the butcher's for twenty minutes to tell me all about Lily's favorite books and how to surprise her with stories. Aaron from the convenience store told me all the details about her favorite snacks and how often she comes in for bottles of wine.

Heather at the pharmacy warned me that breaking Lily's heart would get me castrated and chased out of town, while Frank from the candy store told me that Emma is the key to Lily's heart.

Lily's family is huge. Everyone in this town looks out for each other, and this is no different. While it's overwhelming in some areas, it's rather wholesome in others.

And it gives me a bottomless pit in my stomach when I consider the consequences of people learning that our date was fake. This spurred me to reach out to Lily, but that thought slips from my mind when I return to the inn one night and find none other than Emma at the front desk pressing the stamp against various ink-covered sheets of paper.

"Well, hi." I smile at her as I approach the front desk. "Are you the new hire?"

"Yep!" Emma waves the stamp high in the air, then brings it down onto the paper. "Gotta make sure the stamps work."

"Oh, of course." I nod quickly. "Is your mom here?" I glance behind Emma and see David busy on the phone. If Emma is here, it's not much of a leap to expect Lily to be around the corner, but Emma shakes her head and my heart sinks.

"Mommy's working."

"Oh, of course."

"She's got some big–some big project that she has to finish so I get to come here and make sure only good people get in!"

"Am I allowed in?" I grin.

Emma tilts her head and squints up at me, then she slams the stamp down onto the paper. "Proceed!"

Chuckling, I'm about to head to my room when something catches in my mind. "You're mom's working on a big project, you say?"

Emma nods seriously. "Big pigs in the city."

"Do you mean big wigs?"

Emma's eyes narrow. "No, they're big pigs. Says so on her page."

"Her page?"

Never have I felt so utterly useless as the moment Emma pulls my phone out of my hand, types something in, and then hands it back. The Instagram page on display is indeed for Big Pigs in the City, a butcher shop celebrating its sixtieth anniversary.

"Big pigs," Emma states firmly. "Mommy's making them their fancy cake." She climbs up onto the counter and leans over my arm, then taps a few buttons and pulls up the page for Sweet Noel. A half-second of scrolling and Emma brings up some pictures of a half-finished pig made entirely out of cake. Lily poses in the picture with an icing mustache, and I can't help but laugh.

"Wow, that's amazing. That whole pig is a cake?"

"Mmmhmm. Mommy's also making sugar snap bacon. I got to taste test!" Emma slides carefully back into her seat and returns to her stamping while I scroll through the account.

The page is filled with mouthwatering desserts, cakes, and designs that are almost hard to believe are edible. There's an entire toaster that looks so real until the next picture shows Lily cutting into it with a large knife. Back when I knew Lily, cooking was her passion. She'd talk animatedly about her dreams of becoming a top chef, and cake decorating was only a hobby, a way to disconnect from the stress of the kitchen.

It's amazing to see that hobby become a career for her.

"Well, thank you for showing me," I say to Emma. "I know exactly who to reach out to the next time I need a fancy cake to celebrate something. Or a youngster to help me with my phone, apparently."

I'd never considered myself unskilled with social media, but it barely factors into my life other than seeking out websites on a browser. It never occurred to me to find Lily on social media.

Suddenly, the outer door swings open. At first, I barely spare the man a glance Until I recognize him. Just as I do, Emma slides off her chair and runs to him with a cheer.

It's the man from the bakery. The one I saw hugging Lily. The way Emma runs to him and hugs him with a gigantic smile on her face confirms my fear. This is Emma's father. It's got to be.

"Hey, sport. I'm here to pick you up. Your mom's gonna be working later than she intended but she wants me to bring you to the bakery, sound good?"

"Okay!" Emma nods quickly, but something prevents me from leaving.

"I'm sorry, who are you?" I ask, approaching the man.

"I'm Mark. Who are you?"

"Sorry, I just… I know Lily, and I know Emma, but I don't know you and I'm not sure how comfortable I am with your just coming in here and taking Emma."

"He's a teacher!" Emma declares with adorable innocence, and I would maybe let this go if I weren't desperate to get some clue as to who this man really is.

"Lily and I go way back," Mark says, and his face stiffens. "Call her if you don't believe me."

I hesitate. I don't have her number and had been planning on asking her father to give it to me, or using the number for Sweet Noel after I'd Googled what it was.

"I'm not trying to accuse you of anything," I reply stiffly. "It's just strange to me because I don't know you."

"And I don't know you, pal," Mark snaps. "Who the hell are you, anyway?"

"It doesn't matter who I am. You're the one who's wandered in off the streets and is trying to take Emma without even speaking to her grandparents. Bit strange."

"Listen, pal, I don't need to explain anything to you because Emma is my responsibility, understand?"

Before I can reply, Hillary appears from the dining room and smiles widely. "Mark! How lovely to see you. Are you here for dinner?"

So, he's known to them.

Mark shoots me a withering glare, then smiles widely at Hillary. "Not tonight, no. I'm here to collect Emma."

The heavy realization that I may have just accosted Emma's father, someone who would be prominent in Lily's life, weighs on my shoulders, so I head for the stairs and leave them to it.

As I climb, I catch snippets of talk about a daddy/daughter dance that makes Emma squeal excitedly, and my heart sinks.

Fooling myself into thinking I have a chance with Lily is dangerous, but our date went so well that it's impossible not to get caught up in the old feelings resurfacing with new ones.

And now there's Mark. Mark who has the family I should have had.

Being forced to leave Lily all those years ago is the biggest regret of my life.

But I'm going to fix it.

Mark be damned.

9

LILY

"Taylor, can you hand me that tray?"

Perched on the edge of the display table, it takes all my strength to keep my balance while holding up the party streamers. I can't be too irritated at whoever decorated this table since they likely didn't know how much space I'd need, but it still irks me.

"This one?" Taylor, the receptionist from the medical center, holds up a tray of tiny cupcakes. Each one is decorated in blue icing with edible glitter balls adorning their tops.

"That's the one. Thank you so much!"

"No problem." Taylor beams at me as she hands me the tray, then she helps me set it down on the table next to me. "These are prizes?"

"Mmm." I strain further up the table with one cupcake in hand, placing it on the outskirts of the circular pattern I created with the pink and yellow cakes.

The charity party is due to start any minute now. Even if I'd been on time, I'm not sure I would have gotten all of this done before the launch. I keep thinking of more things I have to do, and the perfectionist in me is really shining.

After placing several blue cupcakes in a line, I straighten up with a groan and press one hand to my stomach. "Oh, I need to work on my core." I chuckle.

Taylor laughs but she looks quizzical.

"What is it?"

"Well…" Taylor swings her arms back and forth at her sides. "Don't get me wrong, your cakes are super cool, but why would people bid on them?"

"Ouch," I tease with a smile. "The cake is just decoration. You bid on a cupcake, and if you win, you then get to choose which cupcake you'd like. Each one has a small poker chip hidden inside which corresponds to one of the gifts donated by people around here. So, the cupcake is just a sweet treat. The real prize is the chip inside."

"Oh." Taylor smiles widely. "That makes so much sense. I was like, who even likes cake enough to bid hundreds of dollars?"

"You'd be surprised." I resume my placement of the blue cakes. "You wouldn't believe how much people are willing to pay me when commissioning my larger cakes. I like to think it's because of my talent, but it's mostly because of laziness. Those people would never do it themselves, so they pay someone else obscene amounts to do it."

"I'd love to do that," Taylor sighs wistfully. "But I think my mom would have a heart attack if I told her I wanted to bake for a living."

"It's hard work." Sitting back up, I admire my creation. Up close, it's just a jumble of colors but from a little further away, the cake display matches the flower display in the town square. "But there's no other job quite like it."

Taylor smiles warmly at me, but before she can say anything else, someone deeper into the hall yells her name and she scampers off with a quick wave goodbye.

The charity event is already looking amazing, and once the people are here, things will really get into full swing.

With the lights down low, the dance hall has a warm, nocturnal feel. Black netting covered in silver and gold sparkles drapes in loops across the ceiling, weaving between the old, gigantic chandelier that's hung in this hall since the building was built. Each table is covered in gold cloth, with tiny little Christmas trees set in the middle and covered in various colors of glitter.

In the furthest corner of the room stands a gigantic Christmas tree that's positively swimming in blue, silver, and gold lights. The only things keeping the tree from looking bare are the countless tickets tucked into the branches. Yet another small game for people to bid on to win a random prize. The band setting up next to the tree will play for a couple of hours, and then they will have to clear the stage for the auction, which will be the most nerve-racking part of the night.

That's where the real money will be raised, and my plans for the free clinic ride entirely on the funds from it.

Checking my cupcakes one last time, I turn on the cooling rack to keep the icing from melting in the room's heat and head back to the entrance. I pass by the photo booth set up near the door and step quickly past the projectors sending starry constellations across the walls, making a beeline for one of the smaller closets.

My phone remains silent, and while I will be here all night while Emma has a sleepover with a friend, I was expecting James to call. We're supposed to be attending this together as our main *date* so that James can fully pretend we are dating.

Only, he's not here.

He's never struck me as someone to be late, but given his job, maybe that's just the nature of things now. He wasn't treating people when I met him. He was just a sidekick to his father's speeches.

Slipping into the room, a smile immediately creeps across my face when I spot a bottle of champagne wrapped in a bow sitting on the table next to my dress.

Approaching, I pick up the small white card attached to it and warmth blooms through my chest.

'Sorry I couldn't stay, but you're going to do amazing! Love you, Amelia'

Amelia had helped me get all of my cakes here, and she'd helped me set up all three tiers of the gigantic cake for the main display. It was just a pity I couldn't say goodbye before she left.

Putting that out of my mind, I quickly shed my jeans and T-shirt, and in the nearby sink, I wash away any lingering icing or flour that still clings to my skin. Retouching my makeup, it's time to squeeze into my dress.

My skin is clammy as nerves start to set in.

What if no one bids? What if there just aren't pockets deep enough to fully fund a clinic? Am I asking too much from the people of this town?

If it fails, if I fail, will I always be remembered as the fool who tried to create a free clinic with *cakes*?

A sudden pull of nausea rushes through my gut as I step into my red dress. It's figure-hugging with ruffles around my hips and chest to give the illusion of bigger curves, but with my nerves making me sweat, the silky fabric catches against my skin.

"Fuck." The more the dress sticks on its way up my body, the more flustered I become, which gets me trapped in a cycle of hot flashes, sweaty skin, and a dress that sticks everywhere I don't want it to.

Straightening up, I pull the dress up to my boobs and force a deep breath while flapping one hand near my neck to try and cool myself down.

Suddenly, the door opens at the same time someone knocks, and James pokes his head through. "Lily? Are you—oh, my God, I am so sorry!"

He immediately slaps one hand over his eyes, stepping into the room and closing the door while I spin away from him with a squeal.

"James! What the hell?"

"I'm so sorry, I didn't expect you to be changing in here!"

"Why not? Did you think I would get dressed up and *then* set out a few hundred cakes?"

"I mean…" James hisses through his teeth. "No, of course not. I wasn't thinking."

"And you should have knocked!" I hold the dress to my back as another hot flush consumes my body, sending another rush of prickling sweat down my spine and around my thighs.

"Technically, I did."

"You don't knock and enter at the same time!"

"You're right. I'm sorry."

I glance over my shoulder. James is pressed against the door with his hand still firmly over his eyes while I stand here, feeling pathetic with a dress halfway over my body.

"I'll leave."

"No," I snap. "You might as well help me get into this damn dress."

James slowly lowers his hand. "What's the problem?"

"I'm hot and I'm nervous and it's making me frazzled, so my dress isn't going on smoothly and I feel like I'm going to look like a frump and people will only donate because they feel sorry for me!"

James's lips curve into an upside-down smile, and he approaches slowly.

"I don't think that's true at all. The hall looks amazing, and I saw the cupcake display. Is it meant to look like the Christmas display at the town square?"

I nod, ignoring the ticklish way my hair dances over my bare shoulders.

"It looks amazing. And there are so many people here already. Everyone is going to have an amazing time. So try and take a deep breath."

I narrow my eyes. "How will that help, huh?"

"Trust me."

Rolling my eyes, I force my shoulders to relax, but the closer James gets to me in this half-dressed state, the faster my heart races. He stops about a foot away and leans down to smooth out the material of the skirt so that it's not as twisted up against my legs. Then he straightens up and lightly grasps my shoulders.

His touch is electric, searing into my bone, and I nearly flinch away from him. His face doesn't change, though. Am I the only one who can feel the charge building between us? Maybe it's one-sided.

Just my luck.

"Breathe," James instructs softly. He turns me to face the wall and then he blows very lightly on the nape of my neck. The ghost of a touch sends a tingling shiver down my spine.

"James," I murmur, but he hushes me quickly.

Then he blows once more. Cool air dances across my hot neck and over my heated shoulders until finally, a powerful shiver warps my spine. I shudder in his grasp and gooseflesh spreads across my arms and legs as if I've just caught a chill.

James releases my shoulders from his grip and two slightly callused fingers slide down my spine.

I bite my lip, immediately jolted back to the countless nights James and I would be in a similar situation, only he was taking my dress off rather than helping me put it on.

Is it weird for us to do this? Although, out of everyone attending this dance, maybe he's the only one who can.

James locates the zipper and tugs it upward. With guidance from his other hand, the fabric of my dress slowly pulls together over my back as he zips me up. The dress closes around my waist, then my ribs, and finally, my bust as the zipper reaches the top. Then James's broad hands press against my back, and he smooths the fabric all the way down to my ass.

"Better?" James asks.

It's only then that I realize I was so caught up in his touch that I forgot all about being overheated and stressed. Pressing my lips together, I slowly turn to face him and his hands fall away from my body.

"Yes," I say softly. "Thank you."

"You're welcome. Lily, I might not have been in this town for long, but I know that this place is full of good people. If there's a way for this clinic to happen, your cakes will definitely make it happen."

I roll my eyes. "If you say so. Now get out. I need to fix my makeup."

"Oh, is that more revealing than you half in a dress?"

"Out!" I shove him playfully. He laughs and dips out of the room.

In his absence, my heart races once again. What the hell am I doing, acting like some giddy teenager?

Shoving those thoughts aside, I touch up the last of my makeup, throw on a dark lip, and then meet James outside.

"I didn't even notice your tux earlier," I say as I loop my hand around his offered elbow. "I'm sorry. You look good."

"Thanks." James adjusts the collar with his free hand. "It's been a while since I wore one of these."

"Let me guess, you had to order one just for tonight."

"Sort of." James grins. "I rented it, actually. I don't want to own one of these ever again. Trying to be a new, normal me."

"Oh?" My brows lift as we walk toward the ballroom. "Normal people have tuxes."

"Sure, but suits are as common as joggers where I'm from. I'd rather wear joggers."

It makes sense. As we enter the ballroom, we fall silent. Music fills the air as the band throws their whole heart into blasting out Christmas tunes. There are already a couple of people on the dance floor while the majority of guests mill around the corkboard showcasing all items up for auction.

"Does the lovely couple want a picture?" The photographer from the booth steps in our path, bringing us to a halt.

"A picture?" I hadn't considered that part. I glance up at James, and he meets my eyes with a smile.

"It would be fitting, right?"

He's right. Nothing like a picture of the date to seal the deal. "Sure. Why not?"

We step in front of the glittering backdrop. James's arm slides around my waist, sending my heart into a flurry of uneven beats. I turn into him, placing one hand on his chest and smiling widely into the bright lights.

"Say cheese!" The photographer cheers, and then the cameras all flash quickly, just as James presses his soft lips against my cheek.

10

JAMES

Lily captures my attention all night long.

I try my best not to stare, but I find myself utterly attuned to everything she does. After the picture, we walk the event and say hi to so many people that I lose track of who is who. Lily seems to know everyone in town, which isn't all that surprising given her work and how kind she is. People congratulate us on being a lovely couple, and Margret's eyes nearly pop right out of her head when she sees us standing together, arm in arm.

It's fair to say Margret fully buys our fake dating now that she's seen it with her own eyes.

After a full loop of the hall, it's time for dinner. Lily often leaves to check on the cakes that she's in charge of, and I enjoy it because I get to watch her without coming across as creepy. I track her across the hall and watch as she smiles warmly at everyone she meets. It sends a flutter through my heart, and I yearn for her to smile at me like that.

When she looks at me, her smile holds just a touch of wariness that I don't blame her for, but I wish I could make it better. So far, we've avoided talking about the past in any real depth, and I don't know how much longer we can do that.

Eventually, we'll have to talk about how we left things, but it's been so easy to just lean into this pretend dating and act like nothing else is real.

I tell myself I can do it as long as she needs me to, but then she looks at me and it's like she's reaching right inside my chest and gripping my heart with both hands. Every fiber of my being is focused on every detail of her, and it's going to drive me insane.

Willingly.

She returns to the table with a smile, and we eat, making small talk with the other guests at our table. I make sure to hold Lily's hand often enough that everyone else can see. We need everyone to buy the lie so Margret doesn't get suspicious, at least until I can fully squash down all interference from my mother.

After a light dinner of soup and chicken with broccoli, it's on to the dancefloor and more willing torture.

"You have to make it believable," Lily says as she drapes her arms around my shoulders and presses her body up against mine. "Margret is watching you like a hawk."

"I know," I reply, despite never taking my eyes off Lily to confirm. "I'm just trying to be respectful."

"What a gentleman." Lily snorts. "You're still a terrible dancer."

"Some things never change." I wrap my arms around her waist, and we sway together alongside the music. More energetic couples dance past us, locked in vibrant dances that follow the more upbeat tick of the music, but my lack of skill keeps us low and slow.

"It's almost comforting, isn't it?" Lily says, resting her cheek against my shoulder.

"What is?" From here, I can lightly press my face into her hair and breathe in the subtle, soft, floral scent of her perfume lingering amid the warm notes of flour and sugar.

"Knowing that some of the simple things don't change. You couldn't dance back then and you can't dance now."

"And yet, it was enough to please you back then."

"I'm not complaining now," Lily replies softly. "That's why I said it's almost comforting."

"I'm taking that as a compliment."

"Please do."

As we rock and sway, shuffling around the floor like we did even when attending parties with more alcohol than sense, I cast an eye around the room and sure enough, Margret is on the edge of the dancefloor. She watches with a beady eye, but there's a pleasantness about her smile that I don't expect.

I hope we've done enough to satisfy her curiosity, and I have no idea how I'm going to make it up to Lily, but I will try.

My attention drifts back to Lily as the rest of the dancers melt away. For a few long, happy moments, I can pretend it's just us. But that's all it is.

Pretending.

She's not mine.

She's not part of my life, not really.

She has her own life, with her adorable daughter and Mark, who I'm certain is Emma's father. Any time I try to entertain the idea of asking Lily on an actual date, Mark's face ruins that fantasy.

Could she really say yes with someone like him hanging around?

But with such romance in the air and Lily curled into me like this, I can't pass up the chance to ask for more.

"Lily?" I lean away from her slightly. She looks up at me through her dark lashes, her red lips slightly parted.

I ache to taste them, to feel her moan against my lips and gasp for air as I consume her.

"Mmm?"

"I was wondering if you wanted—"

"Lily!" Taylor suddenly appears, looking pretty in a blue dress with green frills. "It's almost time for the auction!"

"Oh! I'm so sorry!" Lily grasps my shoulders and squeezes, then presses a brief kiss on my cheek. "I have to lead this. I'll find you after!"

With that, Lily is away and I remain there, staring after her with my heart knotting into a lump in my chest.

I was so close. So close to one more date.

After tonight, I have no idea when I will see her again.

"Look at you." Margret appears at my side with a smile. "You look utterly smitten."

I wave her off immediately. "Oh, no. I'm just… a little in awe, I think. Lily is quite a woman."

"That she is." Margret chuckles throatily. "Don't you go breaking her heart now, you hear?" She pats my arm and scurries away, leaving an uncomfortable tightness in my shoulders.

I don't want to break her heart. Not again.

The dancefloor is cleared quickly, and the band steps away to allow the auction to set up. Within ten minutes, the only music is from the speakers, and several works of art scatter the stage. Everything from paintings to clay models and even a few wooden carvings surround Lily's gigantic cake.

Several people around me munch on cupcakes smothered in blue icing, and I spot Lily on the edge of the stage. She nervously rubs her hands together, puffing out her cheeks. I stare at her, hoping to catch her eye and give her some distant moral support, but she never looks my way.

Lily walks onto stage in elegant, striding steps, and my heart lifts. She looks *stunning*, especially when she hits the spotlight and the quiet sparkles on her ruffles come to life.

"Good evening!" Lily beams around at everyone. "I hope you've all eaten well and danced until your heels ache. I know I certainly have. Now, we come to the meat and potatoes of the night! I can see a few of you have already started making donations and to that, I say thank you from the bottom of my heart. Every cent counts, and together, I'm certain we can make a huge dent in the funds needed for this free clinic!"

A few cheers of support rise up from the crowd around me.

"Now, you all, of course, are allowed to bid on anything that you see here on stage, or any of the vouchers down the front on the tables. If you're not here in person and joining us via webcam link, you place your bids on the website and Taylor here will be your voice."

Website?

Digging out my phone, I have to ask the man next to me for assistance in finding what she is talking about. The man brings up the auction website and pats my shoulder sympathetically.

"Technology, eh?" He chuckles.

I laugh back politely and focus on my phone. Lily's gone above and beyond by partnering with an online auction website to bring more eyes to her project. Many of the online items are free cake designs and an option for people to purchase anything they can see via the livestream.

This is clearly incredibly important to her.

The auction starts with a painting of the town from the local gallery. I'm not much of an artist, but the painting is gorgeous. It depicts the town square with all of the well-known local shops in the background, including Sweet Noel.

However, as the bidding starts, the numbers are low. I glance around and watch as the amount creeps up ten, twenty dollars at a time. In the end, it sells for $250.

It's a good amount, but pennies compared to what the clinic needs.

Next is one of Lily's vouchers, which goes for $500, sold to someone online. Again, that's a decent amount, but it's not enough. I glance around, taking in the faces of the townspeople desperate for change, but there's no one here with that life-changing amount to spare.

I immediately scroll to my contacts. There's not a lot I can do personally since I'm certain Lily won't appreciate my trying to buy most of these things, but I have friends. Friends with deep pockets and a penchant to go crazy at an auction.

One thing about the world I grew up in is that money doesn't impress, so most spend their time trying to buy the right thing that will impress the wrong people. As luck would have it, a small town auction in a picturesque town like this will be like heroin to the people I know.

I send off a few greetings with a link to the website and wait.

Most don't message me back, and those who do merely express shock that I'm reaching out after vanishing off the face of the planet. I ignore those ones, knowing that anything I say will likely make it back to my mother.

The tide changes within minutes. The numbers watching the livestream take a jump, and as Lily presents the next item, a lovingly hand-carved otter statue, the money starts to roll in. The starting bid is a hundred dollars, and it immediately jumps to five thousand.

Lily stares in shock as Taylor stumbles around saying the number, and a cheer rises from the crowd.

"Is that real?" Lily gasps, staring down at the tablet in Taylor's hands.

Taylor nods frantically. "Some lawyer from San Francisco."

"Oh, my God." Lily's cheeks flush red as she confirms the bid, and then the number keeps climbing. The hand-carved otter statue sells for seventy-five thousand dollars.

You could have knocked Lily over with a feather. And it doesn't end there. Every other piece of artwork, statue, and carving is sold for over a hundred thousand dollars, and the dance hall goes wild with cries and cheers of celebration.

By the time the last tier of Lily's cake sells for two hundred and fifty thousand, she's in tears that turn into shaking sobs when Margret hurries up to her and confirms that the money is being deposited at the same time.

My friends are never tardy. I imagine if I ever go back to one of the functions my mother hosts, I'll hear all about the authentic, one-of-a-kind, hand-carved otter statue that no one else in the world can own.

Lily meets her goal of getting the clinic off the ground and funding it for one year. In fact, from the number whispered against the microphone, the clinic is funded for a minimum of three years.

Pride swells in my chest as I watch her hug Margret tightly, then Taylor. Lily's closing speech is a stumbling, weeping mess of thank yous and love. Then she stumbles off the stage and runs directly toward me.

"Did you see?" she cries. "We did it! We actually did it!" Lily crashes into me with an excited squeal and throws her arms around my neck. "We did it!"

"You did it," I correct, hugging her tightly. "Congratulations!"

In the flurry of excitement that bursts out of Lily with her giggles, she suddenly cups my face with one hand and kisses me.

11

LILY

Stepping through the front door, I slowly close it behind me and lean against it with my keys dangling loosely from my fingers.

What. A. Night.

The auction was a roaring success. We raised so much money that I can barely fathom the final amount, and it's all thanks to an influx of interest online. I expected to reach a few nearby artist groups, but somehow, we caught the attention of people with real money.

People who paid by instant bank transfer.

I still need to verify each of the payments myself, but that can come later.

And then, in all the excitement and shock at the success of the night, I'd leapt off the stage and into James's arms, complicating everything with a kiss.

The presence of his lips continues to tingle against my mouth, and I run my fingertips across my lower lip.

It was a good kiss.

A great kiss.

An achingly familiar kiss that never should have happened. I gave in to weakness. We didn't have much chance to discuss the kiss after the fact because the crowd whisked me away, and by the time we said goodnight, I didn't want to dive into a complicated conversation.

So we parted ways.

Home feels eerily quiet after the chaos of the auction. Walking into the kitchen, I'm greeted by a bottle of wine and a note from my mother telling me she brought Emma home, and they both will likely be asleep by the time I read this.

I immediately head to Emma's room. True enough, she's fast asleep with one arm flung wide, and several stuffed animals have been knocked loose, lying on the floor. I tidy them quietly, kiss Emma's forehead, and then sneak out before my presence can disturb her.

My mother is fast asleep in the guest room, and affection warms my heart to see the two of them safe and comfortable. As I head to the bathroom, I text my father quickly so he knows I got home safe and that Mom is safe and sound.

With the door acting as a barrier between me and the world, my thoughts quickly loop back around to James.

That kiss—such a small thing, yet I can't get it out of my head. I replay how he helped me with my dress and how electric his touch was against my skin. Convincing myself that it was just nerves simply didn't work because he made me feel like this all those years ago.

But then he left. I remind myself of that quickly. He abandoned me, refused to take my calls. He sent his *mother* to deal with me instead, and the horrible words she used still sting to this day.

But that kiss…

Maybe it's the alcohol warming my veins or the delight of such a fantastic evening, but everything else just feels like useless noise. I stare at myself in the mirror as I remove my jewelry, and I can almost picture him here with me.

He'd remove my dress with the same tender care he applied when helping me into it. He'd move my hair from my shoulder and kiss my neck, leaving heat flushing through me like a bubbling fountain.

"Stop it, Lily," I murmur, eyeing my reflection. "You've been down this path."

It was such a good path, though.

Discarding my dress, I step under the powerful jet spray of my shower and close my eyes.

For a few minutes, there's nothing but the patter of the water bouncing off my skin and the surrounding peach tiles, the gurgle from the drain as the water flows, and the welcoming warmth from the water washing over my shoulders and down my body.

I tip my head forward and allow the pressure spray to work its magic against the back of my neck and down my shoulders. Each drop is like a masseuse's talented fingers working against the tension in all my muscles.

Then, it becomes James. His hands gripping my shoulders and working his thumb deep into my muscles. The steam from the shower becomes his heated presence behind me, urging me to just lean back and feel the solid press of his muscular chest. The rush of the water catching on the edge of my hair turns into his breath as he waits to whisper sweet things in my ear—

No.

I can't. Forcing those thoughts away, I turn to face the spray of the shower and hold my breath as a thousand droplets of water pelt me.

It's not enough to push James completely away from my thoughts, but it does let me focus long enough to wash myself the best I can.

Unfortunately, whether it's from my lack of willpower, tiredness, or the fact that the success of tonight just makes everything else feel easy, James returns to the forefront of my thoughts when I leave the shower.

In my bedroom, with the door closed and the lights down low, he sends me a text. It's just a simple thank you for attending with him and goodnight with a kiss.

Does that mean something? Is he trying to tell me something or am I looking too far into it?

I spend the next forty minutes applying moisturizers and lotions, then drying my hair on the lowest setting so as not to disturb anyone else in the house. All the while, my thoughts dance back and forth between the appropriate way to text James back.

Should I just say goodnight? Should I thank him too? Do I put a kiss? Will it be weird if I don't put a kiss? Maybe his kiss was an accident, and he'd hit send before he realized, and then my kiss would be the awkward one. Or if I ignore it, maybe that will be more awkward and will prompt him to bring it up in person?

I feel like a teenager again, trying to navigate a complicated dating scene when it really should be anything but complicated. If he were any other man, I wouldn't be struggling like this. I would follow up on that kiss with purpose, and I would definitely text him back.

My bed is a welcome comfort after spending hours on my feet, but I'm no closer to a decision about James.

If he were here right now, things would be simpler. I could talk to him, and we could work out what that kiss meant together.

Maybe it meant nothing.

Or it meant everything.

I stare at the ceiling, still feeling the phantom sensation of his mouth against mine. The shower didn't help, especially since all thoughts of him in there with me, helping me wash, got me more hot and bothered.

Even now, with cool sheets pressing against my warm skin and the allure of sleep on the edge of my mind, I'm still bothered.

Shifting around under the covers, my thighs press together, and a pleasant ache curls through my core. Pushing my face into my pillow, I shove the sensation away and close my eyes.

I need to stop thinking about this and go to sleep.

But fate has different ideas.

Each time I try to force myself to sleep, it lasts only two minutes before my thoughts are back on James. His pretty eyes, his cheeky smile, the softness of his lips, and the way he held me close like I was something so precious.

He tasted the same—a little sweeter, thanks to the flow of alcohol—but he tasted exactly as I remembered.

What if I'd caved into that nostalgic feeling and brought him home?

No, Lily. Stop.

Another restless shuffle around the bed and I try to realign my thoughts with sleep. It works for five minutes.

Then I lose track, and suddenly, James is in my house, pushing me up against the wall and kissing me with purpose. His hands cradle my ribcage, keeping me pinned while our mouths dance together and he steals all the breath from my lungs.

I can still feel the strands of his hair between my fingertips, and I can recall the exact throaty moan he makes when his hair is pulled. I bet it sounds even better now.

Fuck! No!

Frustration builds and my next restless shuffle kicks the covers around and rearranges both of my pillows before I settle. Only this time, I'm tired enough that James eases into my thoughts within a few seconds and I don't have the energy to force him away.

If he were here right now, right this second, I know what would help me sleep. The warmth of his torso against mine, the sound of his whispers in my ear and the stretch of his cock inside me would solve all my problems.

If he fucked me senseless, I would wake with such clarity that I would know exactly what to do next.

Somehow, my hand ends up in my bedside drawer and I locate my latest toy, a *Womanizer*. It's powerful, with vibrations and a delicious gentle suction that mimics the suction of a human mouth. It's not the same as a real mouth, but in a pinch, it's amazing.

Maybe that's how James can make up for all the pain he's caused. He can spend the rest of his life buried between my legs, making me see stars with that talented tongue of his.

I dip my hand between my thighs and slide my fingers through the slick that's gathered during my wild, sensual thoughts of James. I tease gently over my sensitive clit, and a punch of pleasure darts through me, making my core clench and my body curl.

Turning on the toy, I roll onto my stomach and press the device against my clit with a soft moan. In my mind, it's James.

He grips my thighs and holds tightly, keeping me pressed down against the bed and unable to move while he gives me all the attention I deserve. He kisses my pussy, then uses two fingers to gently ease apart my outer lips. When his tongue presses against my inner heat, I lurch and whimper loudly into the cotton fabric of my pillow.

He praises me, tells me I taste divine, and then thrusts his tongue deep inside me with a groan. I rock down against the toy, imagining his tongue fucking into me and licking at my most intimate part. Turning the toy's power up a notch, James is now paying attention to my clit. The vibrations are his tongue darting back and forth, around and around, then dancing shapes and patterns that I can't follow.

Each touch feels like the first, and my core throbs in time to my racing heart. Sweat prickles across my skin like little needles, and I have to kick the covers off to stop myself from overheating. Not that it helps. The closer I get to orgasm, the hotter I burn. James tightens his grip on my thighs in my fantasy, forcing me to remain still under his talented mouth and fingers.

The rest of me writhes wildly. I roll onto my back and grind my hips upward against my toy, biting my lower lip to mute my moans. I slide my free hand over my abdomen and up to my breasts, groping and squeezing my nipples through my pajamas.

I come with a cry, turning my head into the pillow and whimpering as pleasure rocks me to my core. My limbs tremble, and heat washes over me in waves. All the while, James in my mind continues to eat me out to the point of exhaustion.

The toy buzzes uselessly beside me, cast aside after the final twitches of my orgasm pass. I wait for my post-orgasm clarity to kick in and give me a glaring answer about what to do about James.

I get nothing, only a continued yearning for him to be with me right now so I can fall asleep in his arms.

Damn it.

I sleep soundly after that, tossed into dreams of James and Emma and the thrilling sensation of blowing past the monetary goal at the auction. I could have slept for another few hours but unfortunately, a little after seven a.m., I'm woken by rapid knocking and a bell ringing at the front door.

Alarm pulses through me like a bullet as I jolt awake with my heart hammering. I burst out in a nervous sweat, utterly disoriented, and it takes me a few seconds to realize the noise is coming from the front door.

"The hell...?" Yawning widely, I dart from my bed and pull on my house coat as I head out into the hall.

"Lily?" Mom stands in the doorway of the guest room, rubbing her eyes. "What's going on? Are you expecting something?"

"No," I say. "Can you check on Emma?" Then I hurry down the stairs and reach the door just as another rapid flurry of knocking hits the wood.

"I'm here!" I call. "Give me a second!"

"Where did I leave my keys?" My sleep-addled mind struggles to recall anything from the night before, but after checking the dish by the door, the pockets of my coat, and my bag, I find my keys next to the unopened wine bottle left last night.

Back at the door, I unlock it and jerk it open. Now that I'm more awake, I'm irritated at being woken so rudely.

"Alright! What the hell is your prob—"

The words die in my throat as I come face to face with two grim-looking police officers.

"Miss Thompson? Lily Thompson?" one asks.

I nod jerkily, gripping the door tightly. "Y–Yes. Yes, that's me."

"I'm sorry, but we have some bad news," says the other officer. "There's been an incident."

12

JAMES

I need to talk to Lily.

About the kiss. About why I left. About how things stand between us.

Mostly, I just want to see her, and bringing these things up to her risks losing her forever, but it's a risk I have to take.

I leave the clinic around lunchtime with a promise to bring back a pastry for Margret and head through the town with the bakery as my destination.

The auction last night was an insane success, and all night long I was unable to stop thinking about Lily. How gorgeous she looked on the stage, how beautiful she looked in that dress, and then how amazing she felt in my arms.

I craved more the second that kiss was over, but she was whisked away, and I know I shouldn't ask for more. I have no right to even want more since I was the one who walked away all those years ago.

But it was the biggest mistake of my life and I can't let her slip through my fingers. Not for a second time. Maybe there's nothing between us and we're destined to be friends. That's what my heart tells me as I trudge through the light snow dusting the ground.

A biting chill wraps its cold fingers around any glimpse of bare skin, so I tuck my head down into the collar of my coat and shove my hands as deep into my pockets as I can. Back in the city, cold like this was unheard of. Warmth flowed from every building, and all my family's cars were heated. Even in the depths of winter, cold was an afterthought, more like an aesthetic chased by the millionaires around me who would talk endlessly about a mountain hike in some obscure winter country like it was some kind of achievement.

I'm quickly learning that those people were more pretentious than I could have imagined because regular people dealt with the cold without complaint every day.

I certainly felt like a poor little rich boy the moment the days started to turn cold here, and I still haven't learned despite the snow covering the ground and the heavy grey clouds above.

I focus on being greeted by the comforting warmth and smell of the bakery, and it keeps the cold at bay as I walk. In just a few weeks, the town has turned from a gorgeous autumnal town to a winter wonderland with Christmas bleeding from every available crevice. Christmas lights cling to every streetlight, with strings of color connecting them all like a dot-to-dot puzzle. Christmas trees of all sizes sit in front of shops, on top of post boxes, and decorate the town square like its own little forest.

The Christmas spirit is well in the air, and it may be the first time in my life that I've really felt it. Christmas with my parents was dinner parties in rich, mahogany-filled offices and boring small talk with stiffs in suits. There was little in the way of cheer and certainly nothing like ugly Christmas sweaters or sparkling neon lights.

I pass at least six Christmas-sweater-wearing people on my walk and make a mental note to get one of my own. I want to embrace that cheerfulness.

I cross the town square and turn down the street where the bakery is, only where I expect to see Sweet Noel lit up with its usual golden light, there's nothing but a harsh glare of bright lights and a police car parked outside.

All festive cheer vanishes from my heart, replaced by a coldness that freezes across my chest.

I break into a run, sprinting across the street. Panic grips me and multiple terrible, dark thoughts burst through my mind in the seconds it takes me to reach the bakery.

Is Lily okay? Did something happen to her? Is this my fault for not insisting on seeing her home?

With my heart in my mouth, I burst into the bakery and brace myself for a scene from a horror movie or worse.

Instead, there is only Lily, who leaps up at my entrance and clutches a broom to her chest.

"Fucking hell!" she squeals, and her face turns pale, then it floods with color. "James! What the fuck are you doing?"

"Oh, my God, Lily!" I surge forward but catch myself before I actually touch her. "I saw the police car and I just… I don't know. I was so scared something had happened to you."

I scan her face and every inch of her body, right down to her snow-covered boots. Her hair is scraped messily up on top of her head, and there are bags under her eyes. She's dressed in sweatpants and a loose plaid shirt that's buttoned up wrong, but I refrain from pointing it out.

"Nothing happened to me," Lily snaps. "Although you nearly gave me a damn heart attack!"

"I'm sorry." I hold up both hands. "I was just scared."

"I…" Lily's shoulders slump, then she rubs at her forehead with the back of her hand and pushes some stray hairs away from her face. "I'm okay. But this place…"

It's then I notice the state the bakery is in. Behind me, the glass on the door is broken. The floor is littered with glass shards and cake from the destroyed display cases that line up alongside the counter. The till dangles from cables a few inches from the floor, and all the shelves behind the counter, usually filled with desserts and awards, are smashed to pieces.

"Oh, my God." I can scarcely believe what I'm seeing. "What… Lily, what happened?"

She dejectedly shrugs one shoulder and leans against her broom. "I have no fucking idea. Cops came to my house this morning to say the alarm had tripped in my bakery but the security company couldn't get ahold of me. I'd left my phone downstairs in my purse when I went to sleep, so I missed their calls. By the time the cops got here, the place looked like this."

My mouth hangs open and I turn slowly, taking in every detail of destruction. Who the hell breaks into a *bakery*?

"Is anything missing?"

"My award," Lily mutters. "But I don't care about that. All of this…" She casts one hand toward the destroyed display cases. "The cakes and desserts I made are wrecked. I can't sell them. I'll lose so much money on them because my insurance doesn't cover baked goods. Which…" She puffs out her cheeks. "I'm going to argue about it, but who knows."

"And the back?" I glance toward the door leading deeper into the bakery.

"Whoever it was didn't make it that far. Thankfully. It makes no sense because if I were gonna rob this place, I would go straight to the back and try and haul out the oven or something. That monster cost me fifteen grand. But this… this just hurts."

The pain in her voice cuts through me like a hot knife. All plans to talk about the kiss and everything else instantly vanish from my mind. I shrug off my coat.

"How can I help?"

"You don't have to do anything," Lily says. "I've got this. The cop car outside is just to serve as a deterrent in case the culprit comes back. Apparently, they think whoever did it will come back to take in the damage as a passerby."

"Does that make me look guilty?" I joke softly.

Lily closes her eyes briefly. "No. Unless you secretly hate bakeries."

"No, I'm a huge fan," I assure her. "But seriously, you shouldn't be doing this by yourself. Let me help. Whatever you need. Cleaning, coffee, something to eat? I'm your guy."

Lily puffs out her cheeks and rubs at her neck as she glances around, then she nods slowly. "If you insist, I could use help cleaning up. But don't you have patients?"

"I'm on admin all afternoon," I reply. "And that isn't as important as this."

"Are you sure?"

I set my coat down on the counter where Lily's own jacket is draped. "Yes. Now, do you have another broom?"

We spent the next three hours cleaning up the bakery, and we made a good dent in the carnage with the two of us. Lily assured me she'd taken enough pictures and recordings for insurance, and the police had already given her the go-ahead to sort things out. We swept the floor and carefully cleaned up all the glass and destroyed food. I tackled the shelving and ended up having to break the rest of them because the splintered wood was too dangerous to leave up. By the time the floor was clear, twenty-seven trash bags sat outside on the sidewalk for curious onlookers to gawk at, and Lily had a small smile on her face again.

"I'm so sorry," I say as we rest on the freshly cleaned floor drinking coffee. "I can't imagine how this must feel."

"I'm switching between heartbroken and angry," Lily replies. "I don't understand why someone would do this. If it's targeted, I can't fathom why. And if it's random, then… well, I also can't fathom why." She shakes her head. "Who could do something so horrible? I mean… all I do is bake. I make things for people. All day. Every day. Who would—"

Her voice softens and she chokes up, lowering her head to her hand.

My heart aches for her and I can't help myself. I gently drape my arm over her shoulder, and when she leans into me, I pull her against me.

"Whoever did this is a prick. And they'll be caught. This town is small. That fucker can't hide forever. And I know this hurts, but these people? The people you strive to help and feed? They'll help you. I'm sure of it. We'll get you back on your feet in no time."

Lily sniffles against me and nods. "I know. I just need to feel shitty about this for a little while."

"I know. I've got you."

We stay like that, cuddled, until the coffee in my cup loses all its heat. Then Lily suddenly pulls away and scrambles to her feet.

"Shit. I have to go and collect Emma. But I was supposed to wait for the cops to come back and lock the place up until I get my door fixed."

"Go," I tell her, climbing to my feet. "I can watch this place for you. And I can finish with those shelves."

"Are you sure?" Lily looks up at me with big eyes, and once again, those nervous butterflies make a fluttering return to my gut.

"Absolutely. Go. Please."

"Thank you! I will be so fast, I swear." Lily grabs my arm and squeezes, then she snatches up her coat from the counter and darts out the door.

I keep busy with the remainder of the cleaning, focusing on the shelving. What hasn't been removed is beyond my skill to remove, and it looks like Lily will have to get a whole new shelving unit installed. I make a mental note to ask Margret who she used to set up the shelving in my office.

Maybe I can get them at a discount to help Lily.

As I drag the broom across the floor behind the counter, the door clatters. "Did you forget something?" I ask without looking up.

"Huh?" responds a voice that doesn't belong to Lily.

I glance up and tense. Mark.

He stands in the middle of the shop, looking around with a frown. "What is this? Renovation?"

"Break-in."

"At a bakery?" Mark scoffs.

"Yup. You think the cop car outside is decoration?"

Mark glances back outside, then gives me a cool look. "It's a small town. Cops gotta park somewhere."

Annoying logic.

"Where's Lily?" Mark asks.

"Collecting Emma. Can I help you?"

Mark's eyes narrow, and then he glances at the broom. "Though you were some hotshot doctor. Now you're a maid?"

"I'm multi-talented. Again, can I help you?"

HOLLY, JOLLY, AND OH SO NAUGHTY

"Nah. I'll just wait for Emma."

"No can do."

"Huh? The hell are you to tell me what I can and can't do?"

"I'm the *maid*," I snap back sarcastically. "But Lily left me in charge, and no one is supposed to be in here without her permission. Unless you want to have this conversation with the cop who's on the way to seal up the door?"

Mark glances behind him, then looks back at me. "Whatever. Tell her I came by."

"If I remember."

"What the hell is your problem?"

"Nothing." How do I tell him I'm jealous? We don't know each other and yet I'm so insanely jealous that he got to give Lily a daughter and a family. He got that with her while I was wrapped up with my suffocating family. "Just doing as she asked."

Mark's lips part as if he has more to say, then he appears to change his mind and just smirks. "Whatever. Just tell her I'll be in touch about the date."

My heart punches hard against my ribs. *Date?*

"Sure," I reply tightly. "Assuming she's still interested after last night. The auction was quite a hit."

Mark wrinkles his nose. "I heard some parts were a bit… lackluster," he says, and there's a flash of anger in his eyes. Then he turns and storms out of the bakery.

I tighten my grip on the broom and bite the inside of my cheek.

A date, huh? Mark may be Emma's father, but that doesn't mean I'm rolling over this time.

Mark's got competition.

13

LILY

"**M**ommy!" Emma gasps loudly as she follows me into the bakery. "What happened?"

My heart tightens slightly, furthering the ache in my chest as I turn to face her. "Remember I said the Grinch came by and messed up the bakery?"

Emma nods rapidly.

"Well, this is what he did."

"No!" Emma releases my hand and runs at a full sprint toward the display cases. Just as I jolt after her in alarm, James darts out behind the counter and catches her by the waist, then he scoops her up.

"Ah! That's not safe to touch, I'm sorry," he says while Emma squeals in surprise. "The Grinch left some *nasty* itching powder everywhere, so you can't touch any of the surfaces, okay?"

"Oh, no!" Emma yelps. "That naughty Grinch!"

"Exactly. And he—oh, no." James gently sets Emma down on the ground. "I think I got some on me!" He begins scratching feverishly at his sleeve, and Emma gasps loudly, then she bursts out laughing and leaps back.

"Don't touch me!"

"Are you sure?" James grins, leaning toward me. "I think I should share."

"No!" Emma laughs loudly and darts away from him, clutching at her jacket as she heads back to me. "Mommy, don't touch anything!"

Thank you I mouth at James, and he nods his head once. That was an excellent way to keep Emma from touching any of the counters until I'm certain there's no glass left.

"The back room is safe," I say, ruffling Emma's curls. "Why don't you head through there for me?"

"Okay," Emma replies cheerily, and she walks off, but not before she points at James with her eyes narrowed. "Watch you don't scratch your arm off!"

"She's quite the character." James chuckles as Emma disappears into the back.

"Isn't she just." I smile warmly. Seeing her come running out of the school was the greatest medicine for the gloomy mood I'd been in since the cops told me about the break-in. "Everything good here?"

"Yup." James pats his hands together. "You're gonna need a new set of shelves, but I called Margret and she says she'll drop by tomorrow with the number for the contractor she used. And uhm…" James hesitates.

"What is it?" An uncomfortable rush of heat warms the back of my neck as I pray for no more bad news.

"Mark came by looking for you."

"Oh." I frown. "Did he say why?"

"Something about your date with him. He asked me to pass that on and to let you know he was here."

"Why didn't he just wait to see me at school?" I ask, then I puff out my cheeks. "Sorry, I don't know why I'm asking you."

James chuckles. "If I had the answer, I would give it."

"I know. Uhm…" I'd been planning on letting James leave once I returned, but seeing how quickly Emma warmed to him, maybe it would be better if he stuck around. "You've done so much for me already, but could I ask one more favor?"

"Anything," James replies immediately.

"I have to get started on the batter for all the replacements. Would you like to stay and help me? Maybe keep Emma entertained?"

"Absolutely." James smiles widely. "Just direct me where you need me."

He lightly salutes me, earning himself a gentle shove as I pass.

In the kitchen, James immediately tends to Emma and they hit it off immediately. While I navigate my exhaustion and the countless eggs for the batter, Emma fills James in on every aspect of her day. From the morning walk, the crayon she chewed on as a dare, and the snowfall interrupting recess, she talks and talks while helping James mix sugar and flour together. He listens intently to her, laughing often and asking simple questions that send Emma into babbling tangents about an argument last week over the correct way to peel an orange.

In her opinion, using your teeth is the most efficient way because peel under your nails is horrible. James agrees seriously and recounts a story from his youth where peeling an orange with his fingers resulted in orange juice spurting into his eye. Emma laughs long and loud at that.

It gives me peace to work while allowing me to listen in on Emma rambling away. Such a thing fills my heart with love, and I'm too tired to be wary. Maybe this is too much of a risk, considering James is

Emma's father, and letting them get to know each other could spell disaster.

But I need him right now. I can worry about everything else later. As I mix and haul bowls of batter around the kitchen, I also try to decipher Mark's weird message. What date is he talking about? The last time he was here, he was trying to get me to volunteer for the Christmas fair at school, but I shot him down quickly. I have no time for that.

What else could he mean? As I pour batter, Emma dancing at the corner of my eye suddenly sparks a thought. Did he mean the daddy/daughter dance? I'm suddenly jerked back to his odd way of asking me out on a date while I was waiting on Emma, and my gut curls.

"Emma, sweetie."

"Yeah?" Emma stops dancing and brandishes a wooden spoon at me.

"Have you asked your grandpa to the daddy/daughter dance yet?"

Emma's face is an amusing picture and she taps the spoon to her forehead. "No," she replies earnestly. "I forgot."

"Well, make sure you do it the next time you see him, okay?"

"Yup!" Emma nods and then returns to James, who takes the spoon and hands her a small metal spoon instead. She taps it against the bowl and beams. I notice James watching me with a strange look on his face, but I don't have time to decipher it now.

I'm on the last dregs of energy and there's still so much to do.

Somehow, we get all of the batter into tins and cases, and then into the gigantic oven. As the door closes, I collapse down to the floor with a groan and Emma lands on me with a yell.

"We did it!" she declares, brandishing her spoon. "Now we eat?"

"Oh, God," I groan. "Dinner. I have no idea what—"

"Leave it to me," James says quickly. Before I can reply, he vanishes, and I hear the door creak open and closed.

"I like your new friend, Mommy," Emma says, sitting fully in my lap. "He's funny like Grandpa."

My heart squeezes and the next few beats feel oddly close to my throat. "You like him?"

"Mmhmm!" She beams at me. "I like that he makes you smile."

"You make me smile," I say, tapping her nose.

"That's 'cause I'm the best!" She throws her hands upward, then settles against my chest and falls silent.

He does make me smile. He makes Emma smile. It's a glimpse into what could have been if he had just returned my calls. When I first ran into him, I was so sure that keeping Emma's parentage a secret was the right thing to do, but now I'm not so sure. We're suddenly involved and friendly. And Emma likes him.

How do I navigate this? I make a mental note to call Amelia for help and then close my eyes.

Embracing James might be the way to go, at least for now. The last thing I need is to sour whatever this is and have the whole town on my ass for accidentally upsetting the fancy new doctor.

As I mull things over, the mouthwatering scent of pizza fills the air and James returns with a gigantic pizza box and bottle of pop.

"Yay!" Emma cheers, elbowing my gut as she scrambles up. "Pizza!"

"Ow," I groan. "Pizza."

"Pizza." James grins and settles on the floor next to me. "Fast. Easy. After today, I think you need it."

We lock eyes and I smile as genuinely as I can. "Thank you, James. You've no idea what this means."

"It's just pizza, Mom," Emma sighs, and we all burst out laughing.

"Yes, Emma. It's just pizza."

"You didn't touch any more itching powder, did you?" Emma asks, staring up at James as he hands her a slice.

"I promise I'm clean."

It's good enough for her and she snatches the slice, devouring it immediately. I follow suit with a low groan as I realize this is the first thing I've eaten all day.

Maybe it's the pizza, or Emma's laughter or my exhaustion, I can't be sure, but the next thing out of my mouth sounds like the best idea I've ever had.

"James, do you want to come ice skating with us this weekend?"

"Oh, please do!" Emma cheers. "It's so fun!"

"Are you sure?" James asks, his brow knitting together briefly.

"Yes." I nod quickly. "Come with us."

"Okay." James beams at me. "Sure!"

14

JAMES

I haven't ice skated since I was a child, but after Lily's invitation, I spent the rest of the night scrolling online for a pair of skates. She told me there were skates to rent at the rink, but I want to impress her.

I'm not sure why I chose to pretend I know what I'm doing on the ice, but I want to make sure the day goes well so that she will invite me out again.

And again.

It turns out that shopping for ice skates is rather complicated when you have no idea what you are doing. From the material to the thickness and curve of the blade, I'm completely lost. Shopping for skates turns into a two-hour deep dive into all the different aspects of ice skates and their history. That, in turn, leads to spending far too long watching ice skating tutorial videos that leave me feeling far more confident that I should.

All I need to do is balance, keep my toes slightly forward, and don't fall. All the people in the videos make it look so easy that I'm sure Lily will be none the wiser as soon as we hit the ice.

When I wander my hotel room to get more wine, I practice balancing on my toes like one of the beginner videos advised, and I'm successful. The wine could be aiding my confidence, but by the time eleven p.m. rolls around, I'm certain I can whisk Lily off her feet on the ice and have her utterly in awe of my skills.

I will do anything, really, to get her to look at me. My heart goes out to her about the bakery break-in, and just a single thought of Mark is enough to raise my irritation, but I will put up with all of that for her.

Lily.

She consumes me. Her face floats in my mind as I drain my third wine glass and contemplate calling in sick tomorrow so I can help her with the bakery.

I can't. Responsibility looms over me like a shadow, and Margret has my balls in a vise. I can't rock the boat at work, but maybe I can visit Lily after my shift and see if she needs any more help.

Glass empty, I drag myself forward out of the comfortable nook of pillows I'd created, and I'm about to head to bed when a familiar ringtone fills the air.

My light heart suddenly plummets to my gut as I glance at the screen.

Bernice. My ex-fiancée.

She's a lovely woman, but we never clicked. I never held much affection for her, never mind *love*, but she's the daughter of one of my mother's friends and our engagement had been on the cards while I was still in college. It was a match made in rich-blood heaven and we were expected to go along with it because that's just how things worked.

People as rich as us don't marry for love. They marry for financial security and reputation.

I contemplate ignoring the call, but unlike my mother, Bernice hasn't been calling as often.

Fuck it.

"Hello? Bernice?"

"Hi, James." Her soft voice tickles my ear and my chest tightens.

I haven't heard from her in six months, ignoring her calls much like my mother's, but she sounds exactly the same as when I left. The single call she made after she found the note calling off the engagement had been short and sweet. Somewhat understanding.

"Bernice." I lean forward and rest my elbow on my knee. "You're calling late."

"I thought it might be easier to catch you at this time," she says. "I hosted your mother for lunch today, and she had a few choice things to say."

"Doesn't she always?"

"She tells me you want to get back together."

I lower my head and rub my eyes with my fingers. "She's lying."

"Is she?" Bernice chuckles softly. "She was pretty convincing. Told me you were acting out because of your father's death, and that all of this was a cry for help. She said you were *days* away from a breakdown, and all you wanted was for me to come to you and forgive you."

"Do you believe her?"

Bernice sighs and remains silent for a long time. Nothing breaks that silence other than the oddly loud ticking of my watch.

"Did you find her?" Bernice asks instead.

"Who?"

"Oh, come on, James. You think a girl can't tell when her man is in love with another woman? Are you with her right now?"

Despite her rather delicate way of floating through life, Bernice was always sharper than she let on. I smile softly and shake my head. "It's not what you think."

"Isn't it?" Her lips pop slightly. "I know we didn't love each other, but that hardly matters in our lives, does it? No one loves anyone except their kids. That's just how it is. But you were different, James. I know you were trying to please your mother, and your father, and every other person who had designs on the great James Anderson, but I could see through it. You were always yearning for someone."

"It's not what you think." I lift my head, lazily staring around my hotel room while looking at nothing. "I didn't cheat on you."

"Didn't you?"

"I loved her before I even met you." Saying those words out loud feels damming.

"And yet you chose me."

"Not exactly."

"Then what is it, James?" Bernice snaps, and the silky softness vanishes from her voice. "I think I deserve to know."

"I was young. My parents convinced me that I was too stupid to understand life and that I had to work in the family business. You know what it's like, Bernice. You have no breathing room. I wanted to contact her again, but she never reached out to me. I thought she was glad to be rid of me."

"Then why run halfway across the country to see her after seven years?"

My lips part but I can't speak. There's no way I can explain the sudden, powerful urge to see Lily that overwhelmed me after my father died. I just knew, in my heart of hearts, that seeing her would make everything okay for a little while.

"You wouldn't understand," I say eventually.

"Wouldn't I?" Bernice says. "Do you have any idea what it's been like for me? The looks and the whispers and the sneers because my fiancé ran out on me? People keep asking what I did to scare you away as if I'm secretly some terrible person you simply could not stand. I nearly told people you were sick in the head just to save face."

"Tell them that." I sigh. "I'm never coming back, so tell them whatever you need to. Make yourself look good, Bernice."

"I can't," Bernice says. "Because deep down, I know I was just an obligation to you, and you were to me, and had I had the guts, I would have done the same."

"Do the same," I tell her. "Do whatever you want to do, but don't listen to my mother. I don't love you. I never did. I don't want to be with you, and I'm not yearning for you. And I know you feel the same." It sounds harsh, but we both know the truth.

We've always known. I just got tired of pretending.

"Besides, I know you had feelings for the coffee guy around the corner."

Bernice gasps softly. "I did not."

"You can't lie to me, Bernice. I knew you liked him and I didn't care. He made you happy. So go and be happy. Ask him out."

"My mother would enter the grave right in front of me."

"Would she?" I scoff softly. "You're the jilted fiancée of James Anderson. I'm pretty sure anything you do now will look good after the mess I've left."

Bernice is silent for a few minutes. "So, you've really moved on?"

"Yes," I say as my thoughts turn back to Lily. "I have."

"Are you happy?"

"No. But I'm working on it."

She pauses, then I hear a deep sigh. "Goodbye, James."

"Goodbye, Bernice."

My room is silent and cold once the call ends. My past continues to creep up, though it's my own fault for leaving that mess so abruptly. Talking to Bernice was oddly freeing, though. I'd avoided talking to her properly because while I knew her feelings lay elsewhere, Bernice was fueled by a much deeper family loyalty than I ever was.

I half expected her to come here and drag me back.

Instead, she accepts my choice.

I slowly rotate my phone in my hands, mulling over our conversation until exhaustion forces a deep yawn out of me. I tidy up, shower quickly, and crawl into bed with a deep, satisfied sigh.

I'm free to pursue Lily. Truly free. To whatever end this path takes me.

Thinking about her immediately gets me hot under the collar, lulled by the easy thoughts fueled by my three glasses of wine. That kiss at the auction is still crystal clear in my mind. I wanted more.

I wanted to take her in my arms and kiss her until we were both breathless and gasping for air. I ache to feel her soft skin underneath my fingertips, hear her breathy moans in my ear as I lavish attention over her neck, and taste the flutter of her rapid pulse beneath my tongue.

My cock swells at the thought, and I groan softly, wrapping both my arms around a pillow and pressing my face into the fluff as I grind my hips down onto the bed.

She would melt for me just like she did all those years ago. As my mind runs, I recall how she looked half in that dress. Inches of beautiful skin for me to kiss and taste.

Does she still like having her neck bitten? She used to love that and I'd take pride in leaving love bites all over her throat. Does she still melt when having her nipples sucked? Is she still ticklish on the left side of her ribs?

I have countless fond memories of Lily bursting into giggles while I was fucking her because she was so extremely ticklish. I smile at the thought, and my cock throbs. Tickling her became a game because her laugh was music to my ears, and she would tighten around my cock each time she tried to squirm away from my fingers.

Sex with Lily was fun. It was hot and rampant and addicting, and it was *fun*.

I can't resist any longer. I take my length in hand and let the memories flow. I know she tastes the same because the phantom of her kiss still lingers on my lips. I ache for the bite of her nails in the flesh of my shoulders as I fuck her hard enough to make her scream. I want her legs around my waist, her hair in my face as I bury into her neck.

I need her silken heat locked around my cock, need the sweetness of her juices flooding my tongue, and I need to hear those sexy, delicate whimpers that would escape her every single time she was close to orgasm. It was her tell, and my chance to drag out her pleasure or pound into her until she shook apart in my arms.

I come with a muffled cry, spilling my seed across the bed without a single thought of cleaning.

Fucking hell.

I don't even know if she wants me, and I am utterly hooked.

Rolling onto my back, I release a low, satisfied groan.

I will make her mine.

I swear it.

15

LILY

"Now, do you remember the rules?" I hold Emma's hand as we walk under archways of colorful lights toward where the ice rink is set up just outside of town.

"Mmhmm!" Emma dances as she walks, making sure to step in all the fresh, undisturbed patches of snow as we move.

"What are they?"

"No running on the ice. Don't skate in front of anyone. Uhm…" She pats one mitten-clad hand on her chin. "Don't kick anyone with skates, and make sure I see you all the time!"

"Exactly." I smile down at her. The rules are simple, and Emma has never been one to break them, but all it takes is one moment of overexcitement and she could cause an accident. I trust her, though, and I've been looking forward to this all week.

My parents, bless their hearts, are staying at the bakery to oversee the installation of my new shelves. Once they're secured in place, I will spend all Sunday filling them and I will reopen for business on Monday.

It's been a terrible week. Delaying commissions and pushing back orders because of the break-in is costing me dearly this close to Christmas. I almost canceled today so that I could work and catch up, but my mom wouldn't let me.

"You owe it to Emma," she said to me over lunch. "These memories are important and it's Christmas! You need to do something fun. Plus, you can't cancel on James."

I've been far too busy to be nervous about meeting him today, but as the ice rink comes into view, my heart skips a beat.

The rink is set up in a clearing just off the main road leading out of town. All the surrounding trees are decorated with bright lights. Colorful, festive decorations and bright stars twinkle atop the branches. The rink is filled with parents wrangling their children into or out of their winter coats, tracking down lost mittens, and lots of laughter.

Emma bounces at my side the closer we get to the rink, and she starts to swing our joined hands back and forth before she screeches, "Santa!"

Someone dressed as Santa is going around handing out safety pamphlets to the parents and candy to the children, so of course, Emma wants to go there first. I can't resist her excited pull, and together, laughing, we approach the burly Santa Claus.

"Santa!" Emma squeals. "Why are you here?"

"Ho-ho-ho," Santa chuckles. "Ice safety is important, plus, I wanted to see you."

"Really?" Emma gasps widely and gazes up in wonder. "Did you get my list?"

"I did." Santa chuckles deeply, handing me one of the safety pamphlets, which details quick first aid in the event of an ice skate going awry. "I needed to give your Mommy this and you, this!" He pulls a red and white candy cane from his sack and hands it to Emma. "Merry Christmas!"

"Merry Christmas!" Emma squeals, and she turns to me as Santa heads on through the crowd. "Look, Mommy, look!"

"I know!" I beam down at her. "That's amazing. How nice of Santa to come and see you."

"Yay!" She hands me the candy cane for safekeeping and we walk toward the wooden picnic tables set up near the food and drink stands.

There I spot James standing with his hands in his pockets looking all kinds of handsome and adorable. A pair of skates hangs from his arm, and I eye them curiously as we approach.

"Hey." I smile up at him as Emma dances into him.

"Hi!" she yells.

"Hey, you two. Ready to hit the ice?" James asks with a warm smile.

"I'm not sure," I muse, pointing at his skates. "Am I about to be shown up by a professional?"

"I might know a thing or two," James says with a light smirk. "I promise I won't show you up too much."

"Mmmhmm, we'll see." I chuckle. "Emma and I need to rent skates, so I'll go do that, and then we'll meet you at the rink?"

"I'll be there," James says with a quick wink, and then we split.

"Mommy, why are your cheeks so red?" Emma asks loudly as we walk away from James.

I duck my head and try to hush her as my cheeks flare from hot to molten. A single wink and James has me hot and bothered, even though there's so much between us that's unresolved. I don't have the energy to think about that today, though. Today, the focus is on Emma and relaxing.

I hire us each a pair of skates at the stall and then find James among the crowd near the entrance to the rink.

"All sorted?" he asks, showing no hint that he heard Emma's loud and embarrassing declaration of my blushing.

"Yup. Can you hold this while I put the skates on her?"

James is happy to hold my bag while I crouch and help Emma into her skates. Mine follow, and then when I take my bag back and secure it across my body, James slips into his skates.

For a man who owns his own skates, he's rather unsteady on the rubber floor. Approaching the ice, my heart leaps into my throat as Emma takes her first step onto the ice.

We come here every year, but this is Emma's only skating experience, and each year, I get the same fear that she will fall flat onto the ice.

This year, she takes to it like a duck to water and after a few wobbles, she's skating easily in small circles.

"How do you feel?" I call to her as she spins with her arms in the air.

"I'm a fairy!" she calls back to me.

Laughing, I step onto the ice and swiftly balance myself. Then I turn to James and watch as he takes his first step.

He boldly strides out onto the ice and then immediately loses all balance and falls smack down onto his back with a grunt. I can't hold in my laughter as it overwhelms me and Emma breaks into loud giggles.

I laugh so hard that my stomach aches, especially when James tries to climb back to his feet and immediately falls once more.

"Oh, my God," I gasp, approaching him and crouching down. "Are you okay? Are you hurt?"

"Bruised ego," James groans with a smile.

"You own your own skates but can't even stand on the ice? Is this one of those rich people's things where you think you know what you are doing just because you spent a lot of money?"

"Uhm..." James groans as people skate past us, chuckling. "I bought these two days ago because I wanted to impress you."

"Aww." There's something so sweet about that. "You've definitely impressed me, although maybe not in the way you planned."

"I think so," he groans. James sits up slowly, and I offer him my arm.

"Come on, I can help you."

"Hurry up, silly!" Emma calls, skating around us. "I want to go!"

"Patience, Emma, remember?" I say gently, unable to stop giggling as James wobbles and flails like a baby deer on new legs. "Here, hold onto the barrier, and we'll skate together slowly, okay?"

"I'm pathetic," James groans, then he yelps and clutches at me.

It takes all my strength to keep us both upright between my peals of laughter.

"No, no, you're just new," I assure him. "Emma, why don't you show him how it's done?"

The next two hours are spent helping James find his ice legs, and it's the most fun I've had in years. He has absolutely no concept of balance on the ice and falls so many times that he declares the ice to be his new home. Emma laughs herself hoarse and shows off how easy gliding is for her.

Not once does he let go of my hand. We skate along the barrier, and after an hour, James is bold enough to try free skating. However, he immediately loses control and goes down with a cry, pulling me down with him. I land on his chest, struggling for balance as we both giggle.

Being this close to him sends butterflies cascading through my gut, and when our eyes meet, the rest of the world fades away into nothing.

"Ow," James groans, sounding very pained.

"This may be the best thing you've ever done," I tease, his face an inch from mine. "I wonder what else you can't do, hmm?"

James rolls his eyes. "You're a menace."

"Clearly."

The moment ends when Emma arrives to help us to our feet, and we resume skating until the cold becomes too biting and our limbs ache from exertion. Getting James off the rink is just as comical as getting him on, but soon, we collapse down onto one of the wooden picnic benches with hot chocolate and warm waffles to fuel us.

"Can we come back tomorrow?" Emma asks between mouthfuls of waffles.

"I don't think I'll be able to walk tomorrow," James groans. "I'm bruised everywhere."

I immediately giggle. "Proud of your purchase?" I grin.

"Absolutely." James smirks at me, and my stomach somersaults. I'm too tired to tell myself not to give in to him. Not today.

"Sorry, sweetie, I can't bring you tomorrow because I have to work, but you can do fun things with Grandma and Grandpa!"

Emma stares at me, seemingly debating whether she wants to or not, and then she nods. "Okay," she says, sipping her hot chocolate. "I can ask Grandpa to the dance!"

"About time," I murmur quietly. He's been waiting for weeks for her to ask, but it keeps slipping from her mind.

"Your grandpa is who you will ask?" James says, nonchalantly stabbing his waffle. "Why wouldn't you ask Mark?"

I nearly choke on my drink as the thought of Mark sours the sweetness on my tongue. "What? Why on earth would she ask Mark?"

Confusion washes over James's face as he glances between Emma and me. "I'm sorry. From speaking to him, I just thought he would be the obvious choice."

"Why?" I scoff. "Mark isn't related to her at all."

16

JAMES

"Do you have any idea what you have done?" Even with my phone on the table, my mother's sharp tones fill the air as if she's right next to me.

I answered her on the third ring since she had started calling me nonstop, and short of blocking her number, I began to fear that something serious had happened.

In her eyes, it has.

"A disgrace!" Mother yells. "A complete and utter disgrace! Her mother is in tears and refuses to show her face at the country club, and no one has heard from her father. He's likely run away to the mountains to hide his shame."

"Okay," I say, lifting the phone back to my ear. "That's a little dramatic."

"Dramatic?"

She screeches so loud I jerk the phone away with a wince. "Yes," I reply cautiously. "Surely, they should only care about her being happy."

"It's not about Bernice being happy," Mom barks at me. "She's dating a barista, James. A *barista!* She's dating the help!"

"That's your problem right there, Mom. Bernice has found someone who makes her happy and who makes her smile in ways I never could. Your focus should be on that and not his occupation, because that doesn't matter. It shouldn't ever matter."

"It does matter, James. How many times do I have to tell you that these things matter? That you can't just decide to step away from centuries of tradition and cast your family out like this?"

"Well, it sounds like her family is the one doing the casting." My head dips, and I seek to relieve the pressure behind my eyes while squeezing the bridge of my nose.

"When I heard you two finally spoke, I thought things were finally going back to normal." Mom's voice quavers, and my heart pulls south into my gut.

Out of all the choices I've made lately—good or bad—I haven't intended to hurt anyone. Running away because I couldn't face the loss of my father was definitely a wrong step in many people's eyes, but I knew my mother would be alright with the people around her. She has a close circle of friends and enjoys being the queen bee.

It seems Bernice's current decision has cast a wrench into that whole plan.

"We did speak," I assure her, softening my tone. "It was a good conversation, actually, and I think we both left it knowing where we stood. It might be hard for you to hear, but Bernice and I never loved each other. When we were together, I knew where her real interests lay, and in a way, I think she knew the same about me."

"That doesn't matter," Mom mutters, sniffling across the line. "You're supposed to put all of that aside and do what is right for your family. For both your families."

"Is that really what is right? Or just what is done and people are too scared to do otherwise?"

"James. I'm too tired to have this discussion again."

"You called me," I point out, leaning back in my chair until it creaks. "Me. Bernice. It's the same thing, really. We want to be happy, and if she is happy with the barista from the coffee shop on the corner, then she has my blessing. I'm happy she took that step for herself."

"So, you won't call her?" Mom asks.

"And say what? *Hey, I've moved on but you're not allowed to so I hope you'll remain hung up on me forever?* No, I'm not doing that."

"What do you mean, you've moved on?" Mom asks.

My heart stops briefly in my chest.

Did I say that?

Shit. I did.

Thoughts of Lily flood my mind, pulsing in time to the few leftover bruises I have aching through me from last weekend. That trip had been a blast for a number of reasons—mainly learning that Mark had absolutely nothing to do with Emma. That and getting to spend the day with Lily and Emma. It was magical.

"James?" Mom prompts sharply with all sadness gone from her voice. "What do you mean, you've moved on?"

"Well… I just meant that I'm in a new town, living a new life that I'm really enjoying with new people. So of course I've moved on." It's hard to dodge a mother who is so skilled at getting answers out of me. "So in that regard, it's only fair that Bernice does the same."

"Is that what you told her? To move on and bring so much shame down on her family that her mother's hair is graying faster than a bear in winter?"

I bite back a snort of amusement. "I told her to be happy. If this is what makes her happy, then as I said, I support her. Nothing you can say will change that. And actually, things would go a lot better if you and her parents just got rid of this stupid, snobbish way of looking down on people because the only thing that matters is whether that man is kind to her. Literally nothing else."

"You're a tornado, James. You just create carnage and then run away like nothing happened."

"Can you tell me, honestly, that you were in love with Dad when Grandpa set you two up?"

Mom is silent for a few seconds. "Yes," she replies stiffly. "I was."

"You're a terrible liar."

"I loved your father dearly!"

"I'm not saying you didn't. I'm just saying back then, when you were introduced and told you were to be together, was there no part of you that ached to be free? To go and do your own thing, find someone you loved instead?"

Again, she is silent. As she contemplates that, there's a knock at the door to my office. I mute my call as Margret sticks her head around the door.

"James, your last couple of patients have canceled because of the storm. I'm waiving the cancelation fee and we're going to close up early, so when you're done here, you might want to head. Best try and get ahead of this thing."

"Thanks, Margret. I'll pop my head in before I leave."

"Thanks."

With that, she's gone, and I glance out the window. There's been heavy snowfall for three days straight now, which I've found to be utterly amazing. In the city, the snow would fall and then melt far too quickly to be enjoyed. But out here? The snow falls and it stays.

Sure, there's the downside of ice and compacted snow becoming so slippery that it can be dangerous, but each morning, I've seen several kids and people out helping shovel the sidewalks and pour salt everywhere to keep the paths safe.

There's a real sense of community here, and this much snow this close to Christmas is utterly magical.

And now there's a storm coming. It was supposed to roll in last night, but according to the weather this morning, the winds got caught in the nearby mountains and the storm was swinging down to the south.

Seems like it's coming back with a vengeance.

"Mom?" I return the phone to my ear.

"—and another thing. Even if I wasn't feeling that way, we have a duty to uphold traditions. I don't know where I went wrong with you, James, I really don't. You used to be such a good, decent boy."

"I know," I sigh. "But then my dad died and I realized I didn't want to die miserable."

Just mentioning him sends a sharp jolt through my chest, and I press my lips together. Not a day goes by where I don't miss him, but I'm trying to be happy *for* him.

"I know," Mom says, her voice softer. "I miss him."

"Me too." I clear my throat, refusing to let the emotion overtake me. "Look, I have to go. There's a storm rolling in, and this town is in a valley, so I don't want to get stuck at work."

"Will you be safe?" Mom asks.

"Yes, Mom, I promise."

"Will you *please* call Bernice?" She just can't let it go.

"Sure," I sigh, exasperated and eager to just get her off the phone. "I'll call her to say congratulations."

"James!"

"Goodbye, Mom." Hanging up, I toss my phone onto the desk and slump forward, rubbing my face. Maybe answering her call was a bad idea, but it's nice to know my ex-fiancée has moved on. I want her to be happy. She deserves it.

I send Bernice a quick text just to let her know my mother was asking about her, then I gather up my things and turn off my computer. As I bundle into my coat and leave my office, I see Taylor has already gone home and the only car left in the parking lot is Margret's.

"Margret?" I knock on her door and peek into the office. "You're not staying, are you?"

"God, no," Margret wheezes. "My husband is bringing the truck to pick me up, then I'm heading home. Don't you worry."

"Okay. What's the, uh… do you have a protocol for this kind of weather? How long do we stay closed for?"

"Technically, until there's less than six inches of snow on the ground," Margret replies with a chuckle. "But my rule of thumb is that if I can drive to work in my beat-up old car, then I can work. But I'll give you a call. Go, James. Go home before you get stuck here."

I say my goodbye and hurry outside where I'm immediately almost knocked off my feet by a gust of bitterly cold wind. Pulling the collar of my coat up to my ears, I duck my head down into the warmth and brace against the wind and snow whipping through the air.

Ice scalds my cheeks as I walk through the deserted town, with most people already safe inside their homes. The storm has descended so fast that by the time I reach the town square, I can barely see two feet in front of me. It's still a little way until I reach the motel, but as my feet slide on the snow and I lurch against a lamppost to stop myself from falling, I spot a golden light.

Sweet Noel is still lit up like a Christmas tree, and I see a distant shadow moving past the window.

Is Lily still there?

I can't leave her, not without making sure she's okay. Bracing against the wind, I ignore my numb ears and frozen fingertips that remain cold no matter how deep I shove them into my pockets and trudge toward the bakery.

Each step becomes a battle as the wind picks up, and my cheeks flash hot with pain from the snow cutting across my freezing face. Closer and closer I get to the alluring warmth of the bakery. My feet sink into deep snow, and the snow-shoveling efforts of this morning's teens are well and truly erased.

Just as I reach the glittering door of the bakery, it suddenly swings open. A hand grabs my jacket and jerks me inside.

"James? Get inside, you fool!"

17

LILY

"**G**et inside, get inside!" I usher James in as quickly as I can and slam the door closed, causing the bell above the frame to jingle violently.

James stands a few feet inside, stamping his feet against the mat to dislodge the snow—not that it's much use. He's covered from head to toe in snow. Even his eyebrows have turned white. I pat his shoulder briefly, contemplating what I could do to help get the snow off, and then I grab his collar.

"Come on, take this off before you catch your death. Why were you even out there when there's a storm coming?"

"I think it's already here." James laughs, sliding his arms out of his coat. "I was heading home. Left work later than I planned, but when I saw the light on, I wanted to make sure you weren't going to get stuck here."

I groan softly, motioning for James to follow me through to the back, where it's much warmer.

"I'm settled in for the night, I'm afraid. All the cakes I lost last week plus the man hours? I'm on severe catch-up duty to get all of this out before Christmas."

"Surely, people are understanding?" James asks, rubbing his bright red hands together. "What happened wasn't your fault."

"I know, but people also want their cakes for their Christmas parties and displays, plus with the amount of money that changed hands at the auction, I don't want anyone to start taking that back because I'm slow."

I drape James's coat near the back door, where it can dry onto one of the back mats from the heat of the kitchen, then I turn on the kettle. "Here, warm yourself by the oven. The heat it gives off will make you forget about the storm."

"Thanks." James moves as directed, shivering as he steps into the waves of warmth pouring from the oven. "So, you're just going to be here all night?"

"That's the plan," I say, moving to make him a cup of tea while making sure my next batch of batter doesn't over-fluff in the mixer. "Emma is with her grandparents, and I was going to try and make it back to them, but the day just got away from me."

"I know that feeling." James stomps his feet slightly. "Fuck. You don't get cold like this in the city."

I glance at him over my shoulder and laugh. "Is nature too harsh for you, city boy?"

"It might be." He chuckles. "When I left the clinic, I could see. By the time I reached the town square, it was like I was drowning in white."

"Better get used to it. These kinds of storms like to hit multiple times throughout the winter. It always looks like a postcard when it's over, though. Beautiful."

As my batter finishes mixing, the kettle boils and within two minutes, I'm pressing a hot cup of tea into James's hands. "Drink."

"Thank you."

"So, why did you come to check on me?"

"Well, the light was on, and after the break-in, I knew I was either going to find you or I would find whoever was dumb enough to return to the scene. Plus, I wanted to make sure you got home safe."

"How sweet." Warmth blooms in my chest, as much as I try to ignore it. Each time we are together, I feel like a teenager again, with an exciting romance waiting just around the corner. And the longer we spend together, the more the reasons I should stay away just seem less important. It's a little infuriating how much fun I had at the park and the ice rink.

He just has that effect.

"And…" James's tone is softer. "I guess I wanted to do something good because I just had an argument with my mother and she had some choice things to say."

"About?" I ask, carefully pouring batter into two trays. "Or is that prying too much?"

"About my dad."

I pause, watching the last drops of batter splotch down into the tray. His father. My stomach clenches tightly as I set the bowl down and wipe my brow.

"I'm sorry, I didn't mean to pry into that."

"It's alright."

"You want to tell me about it?" I turn to him and hold out a wooden spoon. "You can help me bake. It's very therapeutic when you're feeling like shit."

James tilts his head, and a small curl of hair sweeps across his forehead, making him look even more adorable. Then he takes the spoon. "Thank you."

I set James to work whisking eggs and sugar while I weigh out flour and baking soda. It's simple work, since we're repeating the same recipe twelve times for a gigantic six-tier cake auctioned off at the charity event, but it keeps us warm and focused while James talks.

"There was so much about my life that I just never questioned. That probably sounds really stupid, looking at the rich elite from the outside. But when you're in there and you don't know anything else, it just all seems normal. And my dad, I mean you met him. He was a hard man as much as he was kind, and I never wanted to disappoint him. It took over my life, for a while."

I remain silent, listening to James as he pours out his pain into the batter.

"And then one afternoon he was just... *gone*. It was so sudden, it didn't feel real. Like some awful joke or–or some twisted trick. He was just gone, and I didn't know what to do. I still don't."

Despite the anger I still have for James after he left me all those years ago, the pain in his voice is so open and raw that my limbs ache with the urge to comfort him. Just thinking of one of my parents passing away is too much to stomach.

"Deep down, we all know it's coming," James continues softly. "But I always expected it to be when he was old and gray, tucked up in bed. Not on a train to some conference. He just... died, and suddenly, everything in my life felt fake. I'd been going through the motions for so many years, just agreeing to what I was told. Where to go, what to do, whom to be with."

We pause to load the first five cakes into the oven, and James continues when we move on. I focus on lining the next five trays.

"It was like waking up from a dream. I just suddenly knew that I didn't want any part of my life carved out for me. Sometimes, I think I decided that so my dad would come back and tell me I was being ungrateful, but he… he never came back." James clears his throat. "But then the only thing I knew was that I didn't want to be miserable. I didn't want to live someone else's life. It sounds so ridiculous to say out loud."

"No, it doesn't," I reply gently. "I met your father. I remember how headstrong he was. So many rules and unspoken regulations. I can't imagine living like that." To me, it was smothering and it seems it took James seven years—and a death—to realize that. "But I think acting out in the hopes he will come back is natural. Death is painful to accept."

James nods, his head down as he works. Knowing he's in pain makes me feel guilty for admiring the way his forearms flex and bulge as he works, but I can't help myself. With his shirt sleeves rolled up and a healthy color back in his cheeks, he looks so sexy.

Sad, but sexy.

I'm going to hell.

"My mother wants me to go back. She's determined, but I was telling her that I was happy here. For the first time in… I don't know how long. From even before my father passed. I'm happy. Enjoying life."

His mother. The thought of her sends an iron-like tang across my tongue and I bury my distaste in the next batch of cakes. Outside, the world grows loud with the howl of the wind and the patter of snow pelting the windows. The heat from the oven keeps the cold at bay, and soon, the two windows in the back kitchen are so covered in snow that it's impossible to see outside.

It's like we're in our own little igloo.

We work until the last two cakes are in the oven and then exhaustion brings us to a sweaty, tired heap on the floor.

"Damn," I pant softly. "Who knew baking that much so fast would be so exhausting."

"I'm impressed," James says, and his shoulder rests against mine while we lean back against the cabinets. "You usually do all of this by yourself?"

"I usually have much more time," I say. "I plan ahead for things. Well, things that aren't break-ins."

"Have the police gotten any leads?"

I shake my head. "They think it was some teen trying to be edgy or something. I just need the insurance to clear and I'll be happy."

"I bet that will take some time."

I groan softly, gazing up at the oven while breathing in the warm, doughy smell of freshly baked cakes. "Especially at this time of year. Christmas is two weeks away and no one cares about working. Anyway, you were talking about your mother?"

"Oh." James's face falls slightly and he purses his lips. "I guess… if I'm honest, coming here was a split-second decision. I just woke up a few nights after my father had passed, and I just knew. I knew I was in the wrong place. I don't regret it. Coming here was the best decision I ever made. A new job, a fresh start. New place, new faces."

I study him as he talks. His face, while pained, is relaxed and honest, but one glaring question arises from his story. "Why here?"

"Why?" James meets my gaze. "Well… I could tell you that I found the job in the paper and applied, knowing I was overqualified and that I would get it instantly. Or I could tell you the truth."

"Which is?" I wet my lips, and James's eyes dart down to my mouth.

"I came here for you."

"Me?"

"You."

"How did you know I was here?" When we met in my parents' inn, James appeared really surprised to see me. Now he's saying he came here for me?

"I Googled you. Or rather, I reached out to a friend who knew how to find people, gave them as much as I could remember about you, and they found you within ten minutes. Which I know sounds like I'm some crazy stalker, but I..." He hesitates, and his brow dips as if mulling over something important.

Honestly, I'm flattered. I've thought about James every single day since we parted because of Emma. But after how we left things and how he sent his mother to speak to me when I tried to tell him about my pregnancy, it never occurred to me that he would think about me.

I thought I was nothing more than a distant, bad memory.

"You were the only person, Lily. The only person in my entire life who looked at me and saw me. It felt like you saw through all the bullshit and the rules and the glaze of my parents and saw the real me underneath it all. And then you treated me like a real person. After my father's funeral, I just suddenly craved that more than I'd craved anything else in my life."

"Wow," I breathe softly. "I didn't think you even remembered me. You left so abruptly." It hangs in the air, the option to talk about how we left things, the possibility of the entire truth, but James is so pained that perhaps it's too much right now. "So," I add, gently changing topics. "Why didn't you ever come and see me?"

"I was scared," he admits quietly. "I saw you with your family and your successful business, and how beautiful you looked, and I realized that I had been so selfish. I had come here, needing to see you without thinking about your own life. So I stayed back because I just... I just wanted to be in your presence. For me, that was enough."

"And now?" My heart starts to race and a different kind of heat warms my skin when James locks eyes with me.

"Now I... I don't think it's enough. I know it's not enough. You're intoxicating, Lily, and I wish I had woken up and realized it a lot sooner."

"Me too," I whisper. I'm unsure what I'm trying to say, and a warning blares in the back of my mind that it's dangerous to get involved with James beyond what we've already done.

But it's too late.

Maybe it's the coziness of the kitchen, the magic of the storm, or just years of unresolved feelings, but when James leans in and drops his eyes to my lips, I can't resist.

He leans in closer, and just as we breathe the same air, I lean forward too and meet him in the middle with a gentle kiss.

18

JAMES

She kisses me back.

Part of me wants to stop and ask Lily what's going on in her mind, but I don't. I'd never forgive myself for passing this chance up with more talking. The air around us is warm, the storm creates a blanket over everything, and it's almost like we are frozen in time.

Like what's about to happen won't change anything, but it will certainly be worth it.

This kiss is slower than the hurried, excited smooch at the auction. Her lips are warm and soft. As we move against each other, delicately switching the angle of the kiss, her nose brushes against my cheek and the faintest taste of flour coats my lips. A few strands of her hair tickle my forehead, so I adjust my angle again and lightly cup her jaw.

Lily doesn't pull away, and with each passing second, I grow bolder. I press a little firmer into the kiss and slot her lower lip between mine. Kissing her firmer, I gently apply some suction as we break apart, tilt our heads, and kiss one another once more.

Lily curls a hand into the open collar of my shirt and tugs me closer. Who am I to resist? Our angle adjusts as I lean over her, and I have to brace one hand on the other side of her legs to stop myself from falling over.

With my eyes closed, my senses hone to nothing but Lily. The floral fragrance of her shampoo mixes with the warm scent of cake in the air. The faintest taste of flour mingles with the sweetness from whatever left-over lip gloss has melted away.

We part briefly, and Lily gasps against me, panting into the few inches that exist between us. I open my eyes, and she's already looking at me. Her eyes dart back and forth, taking me in, and there's a moment, a single moment, when I think I should pull back.

I should stop this from going any further before we add more complications to the mess we haven't had a chance to confront.

Lily lightly bites her lower lip and her eyelashes flutter.

I'm hooked.

I kiss her again, and her hand moves from my collar up to the side of my neck. As I deepen the kiss, her fingernails curl into my skin and a thrill of heat rushes down my spine.

Gone are the lingering cold from the storm and the brief burst of nerves in my gut. I want her. And she wants me. Nothing else matters.

Lily shifts, and somehow, we end up entangled on the floor with me hovering over her, scarcely allowing a breath between each kiss we lavish on one another. Both her hands slide into my hair and tug, drawing my head back briefly. Her lips press against my jaw once, twice, then she relaxes her hands and I'm able to kiss her deeply once more.

Balancing on my knees and one hand, my other slides from her narrow throat down to the swell of her breasts. Lily gasps against me and her lips part. I slowly tease my tongue into her mouth as I grasp and knead a handful of her breast through her shirt. Her hands slink down my shirt, teasing open buttons as they go until the fabric falls open.

The first touch of her fingertips against my chest is electric, and I flinch slightly at her touch. It doesn't deter her as she strokes across my chest and down my ribcage, tracing the angular lines of my muscles. Her tongue weaves against mine, keeping up with the dance as I explore her mouth until my lungs burn. Heat flushes across my skin and prickles along my hairline. I'm too hot and yet not hot enough.

Lily's hands slide around to my back and her nails bite into my flesh. She groans as I whimper, and I return the affection by ripping open her blouse. I glimpse her red bra for a second, then we kiss once more and I have to rely on touch. The lace is rough against my fingertips as I pull the fabric down to expose her left breast, then catch her stiff nipple between my thumb and forefinger. Lily's legs lift to press her knees against my hips, and she holds me in place as she sucks on my tongue.

I break the kiss, peck her nose, and then dip down to take her stiff, dusky nipple into my mouth. As soon as I suck, Lily arches up into me with a loud moan and her hands once again bury into my hair.

Good to see some things never change. Her nipples are just as sensitive as they were back then.

"Please," Lily whimpers. "I need you to—James!" She squeals suddenly as my hand skims the extremely ticklish spot across her ribs. She lurches with giggles, but I maintain my mouth's seal on her nipple, sucking hard as I tease her. She squirms against me and pleasure jolts through me like a bullet when her thigh brushes against my aching crotch.

I'm so hard, one touch from her and I'll surely explode.

"Still ticklish, then?" I tease in a low voice as her breast slips from my mouth.

She uses the grip on my hair to pull me up for a kiss, and I slide my hand back to her nipple, twisting and teasing the stiff nub. The rest of our clothes gradually fall away in between hot, breathless kisses and needy moans. They create a nest around us, along with several aprons, but I scarcely notice how hard the floor is.

Lily consumes me.

After teasing her nipples to the point of redness, I kiss down her abdomen and blow gently on her belly button, then I delve into the heat between her legs and kiss against her satin panties.

Lily's thighs tremble and close around my ears, and her hands tug at my hair like reins. I drink it all up as her heady scent fills my nose. I kiss and lick through her panties until she's so aroused that her own slick meets me through the fabric. Only then do I pull her panties down and kiss her heat.

"Oh, *James*," Lily whimpers.

How I've ached to hear her moan my name like that.

I weave my tongue through her folds, shoving my face against her so that my cheeks part her outer folds and my mouth can devour every inch of her. From her clit to her entrance, I lavish attention against her heat and lick every silky, sweet spot I have access to. She rocks against me, moaning my name like a symphony that I only hear parts of as she locks her legs around my head.

It's the best place to be trapped.

Louder and louder she moans as her juices coat my tongue, and her taste jerks me right back to seven years ago. I didn't appreciate her enough back then, and now I'm determined to memorize every single detail. Lily gasps loudly and her legs clamp down around me as she trembles, whimpers, and comes with several loud moans.

I remain against her, eating her out until her quaking thighs fall away from my head and I can audibly hear her pant.

"Please," she gasps. I kiss her clit, then kiss up to the rise of her pelvic bone.

"Ask me," I demand huskily, rising to look her in her glazed eyes. "Ask me, and I will."

"Fuck me, James," Lily moans, scraping her nails lightly down my chest. "Like you used to. I need you."

I kiss her briefly, sharing her sweetness between our dancing tongues, and then I pull back and guide her onto her hands and knees.

Lily's full ass backs into my cock and drags a whimper right from the pit of my gut. It's taking all my control not to come right there and then, but she's so beautiful it feels like an impossible task. Lily tosses her head so all of her hair drapes past one shoulder, and I kiss down her spine.

With each kiss, she rocks back against me again and again until I reach the swell of her ass. Then I straighten up, grasp my aching cock in hand, and position it at her entrance. The first kiss of her pussy against my tip is molten hot, and my resolve crumbles. I'm fighting a losing game, but I will do my best so we will come together.

When I enter her, Lily moans loudly and she slaps one hand against the floor. Deeper and deeper I slide, drawing more and more moans from her until I'm fully sheathed inside. Habit has me rubbing her lower back, giving her time to adjust to my girth. She pants, wiggling her hips back and forth with each whimper.

I wait until Lily reaches back for me and then I start to fuck her. Within a few thrusts, she's straightened up fully onto her knees with her back pressed against my chest. Her pussy tightens around me like a vise and in this position, both my hands cup her breasts to tease her sensitive nipples. Lily's head rolls against my shoulder and her lips part, moaning openly as I twist, pull, and tease her nipples with each deep thrust inside her.

We kiss, a messy, open-mouthed kiss where we exchange moans and trade licks of our tongues, but soon, the pleasure is too much. I can barely think and the heat smothers me. She's burning up against me, and I'm willingly throwing myself into the flames.

I fuck her faster and faster as Lily chants *yes* each time. Her hands cover my own, caressing my arms as I fuck her harder and faster, losing all control of my own pleasure. My hips become a blur, and the impact knocks whines and gasps right out of Lily's lungs.

And then, I lose myself.

I come hard with a guttural yell, burying myself as deep inside her as I can. My cock twitches, pumping hot and desperate as Lily moans deeply. It's only when she grips my wrists tightly that I realize she's coming alongside me, and a deep satisfaction settles low in my chest.

We kiss and collapse down onto the floor with soft laughs and sweet, tender noises.

Lily doesn't move. She lays there panting as I do what I can to clean her up with some spare towels and find water in the fridge. She's content in the nest, and she pulls me down to join her just as the entire bakery plunges into darkness.

"Oh, no," she groans softly. "Looks like the power is gone."

"Should we check it?" I ask as she cuddles into my side and rests her head on my chest. I cover her with some of the aprons, letting heat pass between us.

"We should," Lily says softly. "But I don't want to move."

"Me neither."

We stay like that, and sleep takes us both unexpectedly, leaving the last of the cake to half-bake in the cooling oven.

I wake the next morning with a stiff neck and a numb leg from how Lily ended up sleeping on top of me. She apologizes and stands with my help.

"Oof," she moans softly. "You really wanted me to feel you today, huh?"

"Sorry." I chuckle. "You were everything I remembered and more." We dress quickly, but Lily doesn't speak. In the harsh light of day, things feel different.

The storm is over and we aren't in a bubble anymore.

"We need to talk," I say as she pours us both a large cup of coffee in disposable cups.

"I know," Lily sighs. "But… not yet."

I want to press her, but at the same time, I don't want to sour such a great night. Not when I can't turn my head fully.

"I have to pick up Emma," Lily says, checking her phone. Then she looks up at me, and my heart stops. "I'll call you?"

I accept that and leave the bakery bundled up in my coat, cradling my coffee. The town looks like something out of a Christmas card with mountains of snow glittering up and down the street. The town square is a work of art with the trees covered in snow, and still, the colorful lights are gleaming through like stars.

The air is crisp and fresh, alarming my lungs as I breathe in deeply and walk toward the motel.

We really did that.

Lily and me.

It has to mean something.

As I walk, my phone bleeps. I'd left my phone in my coat all night and hadn't thought about it once. I check it as soon as I reach the center of the square and stumble immediately to a stop.

There's a bunch of missed calls and then a text from my mother.

She's coming to town to drag me back herself.

19

LILY

"You *slept* with him?" Amelia's voice carries across the stands to some nearby unsuspecting parents who lift their heads, curious. Those who didn't pay us any attention were intently watching our little darlings dance their way through the last dress rehearsal of their Nativity show. Emma, bless her heart, was a sudden shepherd stand-in and mostly looked adorably confused.

I clutch her arm and duck my head slightly. "Yell it a little louder, why don't you!"

"I'm sorry." Amelia glances around the dark hall, then fixes her stare on me. "But Lily, what the hell were you thinking?"

"I don't know, okay?" Slumping down in the hard plastic chair, I sigh deeply. "It was storming outside, and the bakery was so warm and he was just there looking so good, sounding so sad about his father, and I just… I don't know. We're surrounded by emotionally unavailable men and then he was there, pouring his heart out to me, and I felt so bad for him."

"So you fucked him to make him feel better?" Amelia snorts.

"No!" I slap her arm. "It wasn't like that at all!" How do I explain what it was like when I'm not even sure myself? Sleeping with James has brought up far too many unexpected emotions that I don't know how to work through. Amelia is supposed to be my voice of reason once she gets over the shock.

She lifts her brow and looks me over, waiting.

"I just… hearing how much pain he was in, the way his voice would shake and everything, yes, I did want to comfort him, but then he was telling me how I made him feel all those years ago. How I was the only one who saw him, and he just had to see me again, and my heart melted."

"And you fell for it?"

"I don't think it was a line, Amelia," I scold sharply. "He tracked me down and moved out here, got a job and everything. That's an insane amount of dedication just to fuck an old flame, don't you think?"

Amelia finally nods. "Okay, when you put it like that, it does sound more serious. But honey, and I say this from a place of love, he broke your heart."

"I know."

"He up and went back home, refused to take your calls, and had his mother basically tell you to fuck off. Have you spoken about any of that?"

"No," I admit sheepishly. "There's never been the right time."

"Well, make sure you do before he fucks you again, or things will never be right again."

I groan softly. Amelia's right. I've been caught up in feelings and actions without doing the important thinking. It's just so difficult because he makes me feel so safe and wanted that everything else comes easily.

Amelia's hand lands on my leg as the next carol hymn bursts from the children. "So, how was it?"

I glance up at her to see a cheeky smile on her face, and a similar one breaks out on my own. "Amazing."

"Really?"

"Mmmhmm. His touch certainly hasn't changed, and he remembered all the things I liked. I didn't even care when the power went out because everything was just so… blissful. He took good care of me first and then fucked me so hard my legs were numb."

"What a gentleman."

"Exactly. And then we cuddled and everything just felt right."

"Okay." Amelia drums her fingers against my leg, then she swivels in her seat to face me fully. "If you're intent on this path, we should talk about it."

"I don't know if I'm intent on anything."

"Well, are you going to avoid him for the rest of your life?"

"No."

"Then you need to think about things. The most glaring being—"

"Emma," I finish for her. "I know. I… I tried so hard to get in touch with him, but his mother was clear, and the things she said to me…" I shake my head as coldness seeps through my stomach. I have no desire to recall that last awful conversation.

If I'd done what she'd asked of me, my life would have taken a very different path.

"But…?" Amelia prompts when my silence drags on.

"But I haven't heard it from James himself. And I think that would be what I need. Because I think I'm still in love with him. I think I never stopped, and it was just buried so deep down there because how could I *not* love him?"

"And he's the father of your child," Amelia agrees, glancing at the stage as the kids hurry to change scenes. "That will always leave a mark."

"And it will be the most important thing because regardless of what I feel or what I want, how he reacts to her is the deal breaker."

"Will you tell him the truth?" Amelia asks softly.

I shrug. "I have no idea. It's hard to keep this a secret from Emma, but I don't want to show her a father who wants nothing to do with her. And if I tell him, then the cat is out of the bag, and I will have to."

"But telling him will show you where his intentions lie," Amelia says. "Either he steps up and does everything he can to make it up to Emma and you, or he doubles down and you will know he is a worthless piece of shit."

"You know... not once has he asked me," I reply softly. "Not once has he asked me what I did with the baby. If he was smart enough, he would have calculated back."

"Maybe he forgot," Amelia mutters. "You know what men are like, and seven years is a long time to forget you got some random girl pregnant."

"Maybe." I'm not some random girl, though. I'm the woman he crossed the country just to be near because he couldn't breathe in his grief. There's something about this puzzle that isn't quite slotting together, but I've wasted enough time playing the guessing game over James. Amelia is right.

If my feelings mean anything to him and if my future has any chance of being bright, then I have to tell him the truth. His reaction will be the only answer I need.

"I'm scared, though." I sigh, watching Emma stride across the stage and stomp her cane on the stage. "Because what I feel is so easy. I like him. A lot. And I don't want to lose that, but I don't want to be fooled again, y'know? I felt like this back then and he left. I don't want to feel like this now if he's just going to reveal himself to be an asshole."

"It's always better to see his true colors," Amelia reminds me. "No matter how much it hurts, at least it will be you hurting and not Emma."

Amelia's words were oddly clarifying. Emma knows nothing, and I will keep it that way for as long as I can. At least she will be free from pain if James turns out to be committed to his abandonment and wants nothing to do with her.

She catches my eye from the stage, and her words stumble as she eagerly waves at me, drawing a few soft laughs from other parents. I wave back and smile widely until she gets back into character and continues.

"You're right," I sigh softly. "Of course you are. Feelings just make it all the more confusing."

"I am a bit of a guru." Amelia chuckles. "It comes from seeing countless parental disputes each time these supposed adults come to collect their kids."

"Ahh, the joys," I say.

"So, you're decided? Talk to him first? Tell him the truth?"

I nod, tension working its way through my chest like a squeezing band. "It's for the best. The only option, really. Because if this continues, then everything else will just add to the hurt. I have to think about Emma."

"And if it falls through, I know it will hurt you, honey, but I'll be here to help you pick up the pieces."

"Thank you." I pat Amelia's hand and then stand. "I gotta pee."

"Hurry back!" Amelia laughs. "You don't want to miss the arrival of the star."

Walking the halls of the school this late at night is a little alarming. The classrooms are dark and silent, the halls seem to stretch infinitely in either direction, and there's a chill in the air that's impossible to shake. I hurry down the hall toward the bathroom and quickly do my business, eager to get back to the hall.

I can't get James out of my head, though. As I wash my hands, I stare at the now faint love bites he left on my neck. If I close my eyes, I can immediately feel his warmth pressed against me. It's selfish, I know, but I don't want to lose that. I want to call him up and fall into his arms just one more time.

But I'm a parent. I don't get to be selfish anymore.

Drying my hands, I step out of the bathroom and squeal as a hand comes out of the nearby shadows.

"What the fuck?" Slapping the hand away, I make it two steps before another hand grabs me in between deep laughter.

"Lily, calm down! It's me! It's Mark!"

"Oh." Oddly, that doesn't make me feel at ease. I turn to face him and my heart sinks slightly. His smile is oddly toothy and as his hand slides down my arm, I'm reminded of how oddly dry they are. "Do you usually skulk around outside the ladies' bathroom?"

"I saw you walking and tried to catch up, but you went in there," Mark explains, jerking his head toward the bathroom. "I didn't know the right place to wait for you after that."

"Ah. I suppose there isn't one. But waiting around a dark corner? Definitely not it," I scold slightly, then I start walking down the corridor. Mark falls into step beside me with a wide smile.

"Noted. Next time, I'll join you." His elbow knocks against mine, and a curl of disgust rises in my gut.

"Maybe not," I say, laughing awkwardly. "Anyway, why were you looking for me? School related?"

"I'm not all about work," Mark says, shaking his head. "I wanted to see you, to talk to you."

I find myself picking up the pace, not wanting to be caught up in some awkward conversation with no way out. The sounds of the Nativity rehearsal rise up from behind the wooden doors to the gym and I beeline toward them. Mark easily keeps pace.

"About what? If it's cake-related, you'll need to come to the store because I don't think I'll remember anything tonight."

"No, it's not that. Lily." James catches my arm lightly, drawing me to a stop. "I want to ask you something."

Easing myself out of his grip, I force a bright smile. "Ask away!"

"I was so sorry to hear about what happened at the bakery. Imagine breaking in and doing all of that damage and not even stealing anything."

"I know," I sigh. "It was terrible, but luckily, I had a friend to help."

Mark's mouth twitches.

"Wait—how did you know nothing was stolen?"

"It's the talk of the town," Mark says quickly. "I stopped by that day to help you, did you hear?"

"I did. Thanks for that." My mind runs. I hadn't told anyone what was stolen—or rather, what wasn't. Maybe my parents had mentioned it? Odd.

"Anyway, that's sort of related to what I wanted to ask you."

"Oh?"

"That man, Jason, is it?"

"James."

"Oh. Right. Whatever. Anyway, I know he helped you out at the auction, but it's not serious between the two of you, is it? Because I remember you saying you weren't really up for dating."

My heart sinks as it clicks where this is going.

"So, what do you say?" Mark grins and leans close. "Come on a date with me, a real date, and I'll show you *exactly* how you deserve to be treated."

20

JAMES

Two glasses of liquid courage may not be enough to fuel me through what I'm about to do, but it's all I trust myself with.

Pacing my room, I stare down at my phone. Ever since my mother's daunting "I'm coming to drag you back" text, she's been ignoring my calls.

Because of course she has.

She only answers when it benefits her, and now that she has me where she wants me, she can get cozy and ignore all my attempts to contact her.

I shouldn't be having this kind of struggle with my mother at this age, but my compassion for her grief is very slowly fading.

It takes a few routes around my room to find the path that creaks the least floorboards—I don't want to be called a bad guest, after all—then I drain my second glass of Scotch and hit *Send* on my text, telling my mother I'm coming home.

She calls me within twenty seconds and is sickeningly cheery.

"So!" Mom declares when I answer. "It's about time you came to your senses."

"I'm not coming home," I reply sharply. "You're not the only one who can manipulate someone with a fucking text."

"You watch your language," she snaps. "You can't be serious. Oh, James, I was so hoping that you were finally over this terrible tryst of yours and were coming home."

"I'm not coming home, Mother, and it's about time you accepted it."

"Then I am coming there."

"No," I snap, tightening my grip on my phone. "You're not, and I'm going to tell you why. I am done, Mother. You hear me? I am *done*."

"What on earth are you talking about?"

"I am done with *you* and your meddling ways. All my life, Mom, all my life, everything has had to go through you, and for a long time, I thought that was the way it was supposed to be because everyone told me it was that way. I had to get permission from you and Dad about what classes to take, who to be friends with, what parties to attend, and who I could date!"

I take a breath and move to the drinks fridge, pouring myself another as I talk.

"I wanted to be a vet, but no, I had to go into medicine like Dad because that's just the way it's supposed to be. So I did that. I studied because you told me to, took extra classes and worked my ass off for extra credit just to… what, get a full run to university anyway because Dad knew the dean? Then, I had to spend years proving that I belonged there and that I was skilled and knowledgeable. But I did it because it made you both happy."

"James—"

"No! I'm not finished. You have to let me speak. For once, Mom, just *listen*. You control everything. You were in charge of my clothes, my meals, my education, my entire life, and that was the way it was supposed to be. And any time I tried to be my own person, you would guilt trip me into slotting right back into the place where you wanted me to be."

"James, I only ever wanted what was best for you."

I grit my teeth, fighting the urge to shout at her. "No, you did what was best for you. What made *you* look good. Having a doctor as a son, following his famous father? How *wonderful* for you. It didn't matter that I was unhappy or had other desires in life. All that mattered was people praising you for doing such a good job, and then, when I thought it couldn't get any worse, you picked out the woman I was supposed to marry."

"Bernice is a good match for you!"

"No, Mother. If you had stopped to look or even spoken to either one of us, you would have seen that we were not a good match. We were just trapped in family obligations. But I'm done with that now, you hear? I am done living a life that only makes you happy."

"Your father—"

"Don't," I snap. "You bring him up trying to guilt trip me, and it usually works, but can't you look at yourself and see what you are doing? Maybe Dad would hate me. I don't know, but I like to think he would respect me for making my own choices."

I resume my pacing with a glass in hand, liquid sloshing against my fingertips.

"I like it here. I like this town. I've earned my own reputation from my own good work. I help people here, people who otherwise would never be able to afford the kind of treatment I can provide. I've made friends and I found the love of my life! I missed out on her once and I won't do it again."

"What?" My mother's tone changes, but I'm mid-rant, so I barely notice.

"I want to live a life I enjoy, not one that's been bookmarked until the day I die. I want to take hold of everything that makes me happy and embrace it because life is short, and I don't want to die unhappy on a train toward a meeting that was planned out years in advance."

"James!" Mom raises her voice, finally silencing my tirade. "Will you listen to yourself? You are spewing nonsense! Are you drunk?"

I glance down at my glass. "Not drunk, but yeah, I needed a little courage to confront you. What does that say about our relationship, huh?"

"I knew it. You're drunk, and you don't know what you're saying. I should have known."

"No! Don't discredit my feelings just because I've had a drink. You always do this! You always find a way to twist things and disregard what I'm saying like it's not important. And that hurts. I want you to hear me, Mom."

"I hear you," she snaps. "I hear that grief has led you down a ridiculous path and you have no idea what you are doing or what you are saying. I hear that your life is in shambles chasing some fairytale that doesn't exist, and if you have any love for me, any at all, then you will stop this foolishness right now and come home."

"See?" I laugh softly. "It's not about whether I love you or not. Because I do. You're my mom. I just don't *like* you. This is *my* life, Mom. *My* choice. And if you want to be in it, you need to respect my choice."

I end the call just as she yells my name, and when she calls back, I quickly block her number.

Silence falls.

My racing heart suddenly pounds against my ribcage, and I sink down onto my bed. My hands tremble, my legs shake, and my gut twists.

I finally said it.

All the things I wanted to say.

I finally did it.

I expect I'll be written out of the will within a week, but I don't care.

It's worth it.

Emotion stings warm behind my eyes as I stare down at my silent phone, listening to the painful thump of my own heart. I don't expect Mom to take all of this without some kind of repercussion, but whether it's the adrenaline from the argument or the alcohol—I'm not sure—I feel great.

Free.

Confident.

My next call is Lily. She answers on the sixth ring.

"Yes, yes, you can do my hair after, but I'm not sure a hair salon should be using *spaghetti hopes* as coloring, y'know?" Lily says distantly, then she's loud in my ear. "Hello?"

"Lily?"

"James! Is everything alright? You sound breathless."

"Everything is great, I think. I want to ask you something, Lily."

"Shoot."

"Come out with me on a date."

"Is Margret giving you hassle again?"

"No, Lily, come out on a real date with me, one that isn't fake and pretend because honestly? I'm falling for you—or maybe I never stopped falling for you—and I'm having an absolute blast. I want to spend time treating you on a real date so please, say yes. Come out with me."

There's a moment of silence broken by the distant clatter of toys. Then Lily speaks and I can hear the smile in her voice.

"Alright. Yes. Let's do it."

21

LILY

"Are you going to press charges?" Amelia asks, her face weaving in and out of our FaceTime call as she dresses quickly.

"Charges?"

"Against Mark?"

"Oh." I snort softly, focusing on sliding a silver earring into place. "I don't know, but honestly, who tries to ask someone out on a date with a cake topper they *stole* when breaking into their bakery?"

"An idiot," Amelia mutters.

"I can't believe he thought that would work. Did he imagine that I'd be so swept off my feet that he used a *cake* topper, because I'm a baker, that I'd forgive him for trashing my business?"

"I suppose his grand plan was to sweep in and help you clean up the mess, making him look irresistible and helpful. And instead, good old James got there first."

"Cops weren't kidding when they said the culprit returns to the scene of the crime," I murmur, sliding the next earring in. I still can't fathom how Mark saw that conversation going any other way. The moment he'd pulled out that cake topper, none of his lies about where he got it held any merit since all my cake toppers are unique to their cakes.

He'd broken into my bakery, trashed the place, and then somehow hoped I would still view him in a romantic light.

Just thinking it over makes me laugh. Better that than to cry.

"I saw him today at the end of the Nativity show," Amelia says, dabbing purple onto her lips. "He couldn't look me in the eye."

"No wonder," I reply. "Well, it's up to the cops now. I told them I didn't care. I just wanted it over with. On the plus side, having his confession will make it easier for my insurance to come through."

"Ooh, and then you can treat yourself?" Amelia waggles her brows.

"No, then I can pay off the shelves and the new door at the bakery."

"Damn. So responsible." Amelia sighs. "Right, I'm away to my Christmas party. Have a nice date!" She winks at me, blows a kiss, and ends the call.

I roll my eyes and blow a kiss back just as the screen goes dark.

My date.

When James called asking to take me out on a real date, with real intention, I'd said yes because it would be the perfect opportunity for us to talk. I hadn't expected him to then turn up at my home with a bag full of ingredients and a promise to cook for me.

"You bake all day," he'd said, setting the bags down in the kitchen. "Let me create something for you."

When Emma ran up to him for a hug and demanded help, I couldn't say no. So right now, James is in my kitchen cooking me dinner alongside my daughter.

In another life, this would be a regular occurrence. Facing the truth of what we need to talk about will be difficult with Emma around, but once she goes to sleep, I'm certain I'll be able to express all the things I need to say.

That mental confidence does nothing to untangle the nest of snakes in my gut as I head downstairs wearing a soft green dress that flows about my knees as I walk. A sweet and spicy scent fills the air when I approach the kitchen, and when I poke my head inside, I'm met with a delightful sight.

Emma stands on her stool with a hat made of paper on her head declaring her the *Head Chef*. It slants to one side as she ducks her head and focuses on stirring a saucepan. James is nearby, dancing along to the soft Christmas music that plays from his phone while he spins tortilla wraps around in his hands.

"How's the sauce looking, Chef?"

"Tasty!" Emma declares with a lick of the spoon. "You did good."

"Why, thank you." James laughs. "Although, try not to eat it all before we put it in the pan."

"Taste testing is important. Mommy says so," Emma says matter-of-factly.

"That's true," James agrees, swaying back and forth. "But it's so good you won't want to stop."

He's right, and as she dips the spoon into the pot again, James sweeps her off the stool with one arm. Emma squeals and laughs, yelling as he spins her around and sets her down on the second stool in front of the tray.

"Sorry, Head Chef, but you're required over here!"

"What do I do?" She looks up at him with such trust that my heart squeezes. I've seen them together before, but right in this moment, they're so painfully father and daughter it's a wonder James doesn't already know.

I remain silent, watching as James guides her through how to fill the wraps with a spoonful of the mixture, a sprinkle of cheese, and then how to fold them over. They're on their third one when Emma finally notices me.

"Mommy! You look so nice!"

James's head snaps up and he smiles warmly when our eyes meet. "You do. You look amazing."

"Thank you." Warmth rushes to my cheeks. "So, what have my two master chefs been making tonight?"

"Enlidas!" Emma declares.

"Enchiladas," James corrects with a laugh. "Ten minutes in the oven and they will be ready to eat." He sweeps the full tray away from Emma and slides it into the oven.

"They smell amazing already," I say as I fall into old habits and start to clean up. I only manage to get one swipe of the cloth before James snatches it from me and flicks his tongue against his teeth.

"Not you. You are being treated tonight, so please, go and sit at the table and let me clean up."

"James—"

"I insist! Go! Shoo!" He flaps his hands, and I obey, laughing.

It's nice to be treated like this. I don't think I ever have been before. Emma discards her hat and scurries over to me, climbing into the chair next to me. As she begins to tell me about how amazing her Nativity show was and how excited she is to do it again tomorrow night, I watch James bustle around out of the corner of my eye.

He fits in almost too well, like he's been cooking in that kitchen for years. I know Emma likely told him where everything was, but he finds it all with ease and the softer side of my heart eats up the domesticity of it. Especially with Emma chatting away happily beside me. My heart is just melting.

When dinner is served, James sits on the other side of me, and our knees bump together under the table. I enjoy the contact so I don't move away, and we dig into what is, unknowingly, our first family meal.

"Wow," I moan softly. "I didn't know you could cook."

"I'm exceptional with my hands." James smiles. "Do I look like I can't cook?"

"I mean, aren't you more used to people cooking for you?" I say with a smile. "I'm impressed, that's all."

"It's yummy!" Emma declares, stabbing at her food like she's trying to kill the already dead chicken. "I love it! Better than the nasty, dusty biscuits Mark made that time."

"Oh, God." I groan at the memory of him dropping round with his family recipe biscuits long before I knew he was interested in me. Those biscuits were certainly something.

"I'm glad." James chuckles. "Simple and easy but oh, so tasty."

We eat amicably and share stories of our days. Mine was filled with baking the last cake I was behind on and sending two more away to those who won the baking tickets at the auction. James keeps his details light but had a busy day with patients, and Emma happily tells us all about her third day in the Nativity. Each night has been a success and she only has one left to go.

After dinner, James serves ice cream and we retire to the lounge, where we watch some Christmas cartoons until bedtime rolls around for Emma. With all the excitement of James and dinner, I expect her to stay up later, but as soon as her eyes droop, she's ready for bed. I excuse us and take care of getting her into bed, tucking her in with several kisses and a story.

She's asleep by the time I finish page five.

Back downstairs, James has cracked open a bottle of wine and he hands me a glass of red. "Happy?"

"Very," I say, sipping my drink. "What made you want to cook instead of going out?"

"Well, I know Emma is an important part of your life, so I thought cooking for you both would show you that I'm serious about wanting to be in your life."

I settle back into the soft cushions of the couch and watch James as he speaks. The lights are down low, and while muted, the TV switches to a music show that paints light and color over his face.

"You really mean that?" I ask, curious why he means it now when back then, it was so easy for him to get rid of me.

"I do." James tilts his glass and takes a drink. "You and Emma are amazing. And together. Which I accept. No one can date you without making friends with Emma."

Does he really not know? Is he really unable to connect the dots between seven years ago and now?

"That's true," I reply.

"And Mark?" James snorts, and there's a smug look in his eye. "I heard he was in a spot of bother."

"Did you hear the details?"

"Nope, but Margret told me it involved you and she wants me to get the details."

I tip my head back and laugh. "Mark was the one who broke into my bakery and destroyed it. His grand plan was to be my knight in shining armor. He was just late. And stupid. He asked me out with one of my own cake toppers. I suppose it was meant to be romantic."

"Wow," James breathes and he slides closer. "Are you okay?"

"What do you mean?"

"Can't be easy learning someone you trusted broke into your business like that."

"I wouldn't say I trusted him," I correct gently. "But I don't know. I'm just happy to have answers. And to get insurance moving. I'm sure I'll be laughing about it soon."

"No wonder he was so annoyed at me that day he turned up, trying to be all cagey." James rolls his eyes and takes another drink. "I'm happy to benefit from his terrible plan, though. Getting to spend time with you?" James winks. "I'll take all the chances I can get."

I should ask him. I should put down my glass and ask him why he left. Why he had his mother speak to me that way all those years ago.

But the words don't come.

This night has been lovely. Good food, excellent company, and a happy Emma make for a happy Lily.

I don't want to ruin this. Putting it off can't be a good idea, but I don't have the heart to bring it up right now. Not when my skin is warm, my blood is heated, and my attention keeps drifting down to James's silk shirt, which has three buttons open near his collar.

Tomorrow. I can ask him tomorrow.

I set my glass side and move closer on the couch. James's attention is on me completely, and his eyes dart down to my lips, then back to my eyes.

"James," I say softly. "We should talk."

"We should," he says huskily, eyeing my lips again.

"But this has been such a nice night. I've never had someone cook for me before."

"You're welcome," James says. "It has been a nice night."

"Maybe…" Warmth pulses across my bare arms and my heart begins to flutter. "Maybe we can talk tomorrow?"

"In the daytime?" James nods. "Sounds wise. I like that idea."

I lean closer. "Maybe tomorrow morning?"

"I'm free," James says, and his voice is low.

I should resist.

I don't.

I give in to the warmth in my heart and slide into James's lap, cupping his face and kissing him deeply.

Maybe in a few years, I'll explore why someone cooking me dinner, and caring for me, got me so hot and bothered, but that's a job for a therapist.

James's hands settle on my waist, caressing my thighs as we kiss deeply. I stroke his jaw, feeling the light stubble along his cheek, and weave my tongue along his with a soft moan. I'm not even sure what I want fully, but I know I want him.

Both my hands slide down to his chest and I grasp his shirt. With one tug, I pull it open and a sudden rise of hardness beneath me makes me pull back and glance down.

"Are you hard already?"

"Sorry," James gasps, and his cheeks flush pink. "You're just so *hot*."

"Wow." I smile, and pride swells in my chest. Have I ever turned someone on just from a kiss? "You'd better put that thing to use."

22

JAMES

"Is it really so hard to believe?" I say, looking deep into her eyes. "You turn me on with just a touch, Lily. I can't describe how utterly enamored I am with you, but please believe me, the power you have over me needs to be studied."

Lily laughs, a delightful sound that sends my heart racing. I want to pick her up, throw her down onto the couch, and ravish her but when I try, Lily whines in complaint.

She wants to remain on top.

I can work with that.

As we kiss lazily, I slide one hand under her dress and seek out her panties, only to find that she isn't wearing any. My hand pauses against the heat of her pussy and I break the kiss.

"Madam, where did your underwear go?"

Lily smirks at me, caressing my cheek with the backs of her fingers. "I think I lost them when I was upstairs."

"You poor thing," I murmur, sliding two fingers through her silken heat. "I'll take care of you."

Lily's head tips back and she rocks upward, giving me space to slide my hand underneath her. When she rocks back down, I slide two fingers deep inside her and she moans softly. Her hands drop to my shoulders, and she starts to rock repeatedly on my fingers. I meet her thrusts with twists of my thumb across her clit.

My free hand slides across her shoulder, and I cup her neck, guiding her in for another kiss. Our tongues weave and dance together. I bite her lower lip and then break the kiss to lavish attention down her throat. Her pulse flutters against my tongue as I kiss her neck, whispering sweet praise against her hot skin, all the while gently fucking her with my fingers.

Lily comes with a gentle cry that she muffles by dipping her head forward and burying against my shoulder. I cradle her through each tremble of pleasure, but I don't stop there.

As soon as she takes a breath, we work together to free my cock from my pants, and Lily takes the lead once more. She positions herself over my cock, then sinks down with a long, low moan.

"Oh, shit," she gasps. "Still as huge as ever."

"It's not been that long since the last time." I laugh softly. "I didn't shrink."

"Imagine." Lily giggles, moaning again. "Oh, fuck, that's it." She doesn't rest until she's fully seated and her fingers dig sharply into my shoulders.

"Comfy?" I tease, then I gasp and jerk forward and Lily clenches her muscles down around my cock.

"Very," she whimpers. "You?"

"Heaven."

Grasping a handful of her hair, I drag her down for a kiss and she starts to move. Lily lifts herself up slowly, then lets her weight drop her back down with a whimper. I kiss her deeply, then return to her neck and kiss down to the valley of her breasts. As she rises and falls against me, I pull her dress down to expose her gorgeous breasts and take each in hand.

"Yes," Lily moans, throwing her head back. "Just like that... right there!"

Teasing one nipple with one hand, I take her other breast into my mouth and use my tongue and teeth to worship her. One arm winds around her waist to keep her close to me and provide stability while she bounces, and it's growing harder and harder to keep my pleasure at bay.

Just like last time, everything about Lily drives me to the edge faster than I'd like. I want to spend every second with her, exploring and experiencing her, but my cock has other ideas. Every single one of her moans is like music to my ears. Her pussy grips me so tightly, it's hard to believe we weren't crafted for one another, and each time she scratches her nails down my shoulders, it's like pure liquid pleasure straight to my core.

"Lily," I gasp, letting my head fall back against the couch.

"Mmm?" She tosses her head, letting her hair drape over one shoulder like a curtain. When she leans over to kiss me, it tickles my bare shoulder and I shudder.

"You're amazing."

"I know," Lily purrs. She braces her hands against my chest and then, suddenly, it's like I don't matter.

Lily falls into her own world, this picture of beauty rocking her head back and forth as she works herself up and down my cock. I'm here for her pleasure, and only her pleasure.

I dig it.

I keep my hands on her hips for balance, but she doesn't need it. Lily is in control until the moment she reaches the cusp of her pleasure, and when she comes, her entire face lights up like stars have descended.

Her whimpers and gasps wash over me as my own orgasm crests, and I spill myself deep inside her with a grunt. Lily's head finally falls forward, and forehead to forehead, she pants against me with a grin.

"Wow," she croaks.

"I'm not done," I say. Now that she's trembling and limp from her second orgasm, I switch our positions and continue to fuck her for a few more thrusts until I soften. Then I slip free and disappear down between her thighs to pleasure her to her next orgasm.

By the time she comes, Lily is a gasping, trembling mess who can barely keep a grip on my hair. She lazily pats my cheek, gasping and moaning into my mouth as we lazily kiss and the last trickles of pleasure sink into her bones.

"Best date ever," Lily whispers, suckling on my lower lip as the kiss breaks. "You wanna stay the night?"

"Thought you'd never ask."

We stay there, tangled together, until the early morning hours. Once sensation returns to our legs, Lily leads me upstairs and we share an intimate shower together. I wash her hair and she washes my body, and then we hold one another under the pouring hot spray.

Tomorrow. We will talk tomorrow.

When Lily pulls me into her bed and cuddles up to me, nothing else in the world matters. This is where I want to be.

Where I should have been these past seven years.

Such wasted time that I will do anything to make up for it.

Sleep takes me, and I tumble into warm dreams full of Lily and contentment until a strange banging wakes me. I jolt awake, finding the bed empty and the air around me cold.

"Lily?" I call, squinting at the clock. It's just after eight in the morning. Sliding from the bed, I dress quickly because I don't want Emma to see me in any kind of state of undress, then I slip from the room.

Something clatters in the kitchen, and I head down to investigate but halfway there, a familiar voice drifts to meet me with words that turn me to stone.

"You harlot! You know he's engaged, don't you?"

23

LILY

The most alarming thing about having someone pound on my door at eight in the morning wasn't that I spilled coffee all over the counter but that I was only half-dressed because I'd planned on returning to bed and snuggling with James.

That plan goes right out the window when I open my door and a short woman shoves past me and storms into my home.

"Excuse me!" I gasp, struggling to keep my house coat wrapped around me. The door remains ajar as I follow the woman through to my lounge where she glances around and then storms into my kitchen. The moment she sees the spilled coffee, she scoffs bitterly and spins to face me.

"Well?" she demands. "Where is he, hmm?"

I am stunned. I've never seen this woman before in my life and she stands before me like she leaped from the pages of one of those lifestyle magazines. Her tightly curled, sandy hair peeks out from beneath a small hat covered in flowers. She wears a slim red dress and dark tights with a string of pearls nestled among ruffled fabric along her neckline. She clutches a shining black leather bag between her hands, and her makeup is immaculate, if slightly powdery. With rosy cheeks from the cold and a tight, pursed, upside-down smile, I feel like I'm about to get the scolding of a lifetime.

"I'm sorry, who the hell are you? How dare you just come storming into my house like this? I'll ask you once to get back outside before I call the police!"

"Oh, that won't help you, dear," the woman scoffs. "I know he is here. You can't hide him from me. Enough is enough, you hear? I have had it up to here with all the lying and the sneaking and the pretending. This is over, you understand me?"

"Lady, I have no idea what on earth you are talking about!"

"And this is the house you keep?" She casts her judgmental gaze over the coffee spill.

A punch of shame worms through my chest and I dart forward, grabbing paper towels as I go. Why I'm letting some stranger make me feel judged in my own home, I have no idea, but in just a few words, she makes me feel like I need to deep clean my home from roof to cellar.

"Listen, you'd better start explaining yourself or I'm calling the police."

"Adultery should be an offense," she snaps. "I know women like you. Can't find a man of your own so you go sneaking around with someone else's, without a thought to the other woman, you harlot! You know he's engaged, don't you?"

I stop dead in my tracks, coffee-soaked towels in one hand, and stare at her.

"James?" I ask.

James suddenly bursts into the kitchen, his hair a wild mess. "Mom! What the fuck are you doing here?"

Mom?

"Don't use that foul language with me," his mother snaps. "You know exactly why I am here."

"No," James snaps, moving to stand between me and his mother. "I really don't. You can't just barge into someone's house like this. This isn't New York. This place isn't one of your estates!"

"I can if I think you are in danger or I'm worried you're not in your right mind," his mother snaps.

I can't believe what I'm hearing. His mother is here? What little he's told me of her is enough to put me off her, but now she stands here, insisting that James is still engaged. My heart races so fast that I can see shadows pulsing on either side of me, and I brace myself on the counter.

"I *was* engaged, yes," James says, then he turns to me. "But I broke it off right after my father died. My ex-fiancée has moved on." He turns back to his mother. "*I've* moved on. Why can't you accept that!"

"Because I know it's not you, not the real you making these decisions. Neither is Bernice. You think she's moved on with the *coffee* boy? Don't be so ridiculous. James, you're coming home with me. I'm not asking."

"No," James says. "I'm not."

It's a strange glimpse into the world James has been trying to escape, and a surge of conflicting emotions rushes through me. On one hand, I'm furious that she's here when my daughter is just upstairs, and I am ready to throw hands if she dares move toward the stairs. On the other hand, I know James has been avoiding her, and I can't imagine how I would feel if I lost Emma in a similar way.

But his mother is convinced he is still engaged and another shameful, dirty feeling washes over me despite James's reassurance.

Am I the other woman?

As James and his mother argue, it quickly becomes clear that I'm not the other woman. His mother is just unable to let go of the engagement for some absurd reason.

"James, think about this seriously," his mother says, trying to place a hand on his arm, but he moves away. "You have a family back in the city. You have responsibilities to your father's business, to his legacy. You have people there who love and care for you, and here? Here, there is nothing."

"That's the life *you* want me to live," James snaps. "I don't want that life. Why won't you listen to me?"

"You shouldn't be here!" she screeches suddenly. "There's nothing for you here!"

My heart stalls in my chest.

There's nothing for you here, not with him.

Her screech jerks me back to seven years ago when I finally managed to get through to James to tell him I was pregnant, and instead, it was his mother. I hadn't fully recognized her up until that moment, but she screeched at me the same way with similar words when I spoke to her.

I told her it was urgent and she pressed constantly until I told her the truth. That I was pregnant and James was the father. She turned cold and bitter, telling me James wanted nothing to do with me and that I had no future, no life in their family.

Then she made me an offer that still haunts me to this day, and a sudden coldness washes over my shoulders.

I want this woman out of my house and away from my daughter.

Their argument continues and the more they debate back and forth—well, it's not really a debate. James is pretty clear in what he wants to do, but for some reason, his mother simply refuses to accept—pieces start to slot together in my mind.

Why has James never connected the dots about Emma? Does he not remember that I was pregnant? It was years ago, but if I had the impact on him that he claims, could he really forget?

And if so, why did he think Mark was Emma's father?

The sopping, coffee-soaked paper towels ball up in my fist and the cold liquid drips through my fingertips.

Is it possible that he never knew? Did he never know I was pregnant?

The way his mother talks, I begin to doubt everything she told me back then. Her insistence that James wanted rid of me, that he couldn't face me and was annoyed I didn't take the hint… was that really James or was it his mother getting rid of a problem she saw?

The more I think about it, the more it makes sense and all the other moments of confusion suddenly clear up as they slot into place.

James has never once asked about my pregnancy because he didn't know I was pregnant, did he?

I watch his mother throw her hands in the air, scolding James for letting down shareholders and dragging their name through the mud. That's where her focus is. On her immediate family, her name and her reputation. It's clear that nothing else matters to her.

"Get out," I say softly, tossing the paper towels into the sink.

Neither of them reacts, unable to hear me over their argument.

"You are unbelievable!" James barks. "You constantly talk at me, never to me. You are so determined to shove me into some little box that nothing else matters, does it? You're so insane you barged into Lily's home. Look at yourself, Mom. What would Dad think?"

His mother's hand flies out and she strikes James hard across the face.

"Don't you dare," she snaps. "Don't you dare talk about him like that. If he were still here, none of this would be happening!"

"It would still happen," James says sadly. "It would just take me longer to realize how fucking sad I was."

"Get out!" I repeat louder, stepping forward. I glare at his mother. "You are not welcome here. If you want to continue this discussion, then that's fine, but you are not doing it in my kitchen, understand? You are a rude, foul woman and if you don't get out of my home, I am calling the police!"

"Lily!" James whirls around. "There's no need for that."

"Yes, there fucking is," I snap. "There's an intruder in my home."

"She'll leave." James turns back to his mother. "Please leave. I can meet you in town somewhere and we can talk more, but not here."

"No." James's mother stands an inch taller and she glares at me, then she faces James with narrow eyes. "You will come with me right now, James. This nonsense ends here."

"No."

"Yes, you will," she snaps. "You come home now, or you will never see a dime of the family money. I will scrub your name from everything and I will disown you!"

My heart punches up into my throat, caught between furious desperation to get this woman out of my house and shock at the ultimatum she throws down at him.

James glances at me and our eyes meet for a second, then he faces her once more.

"Disown me. I am staying right here. This is where I belong."

He chose me.

I didn't know what to expect. Perhaps James would try to talk his mother into continuing this elsewhere, but no, he immediately made a choice.

And he chose me.

Shit.

I think I'm falling for him all over again.

24

JAMES

"You've really never been to a Christmas fair before?" Lily slowly walks beside me as we take in the fragrant beauty of the Christmas festival that's now in full swing.

Twinkling lights dance overhead like stars, the cold nips at my fingers and freezes my lungs, and the scent of cinnamon is almost overwhelming. But I love it. This is my future.

Two days ago, my mother came to town and demanded I return to the city with her. She provided an ultimatum to my face, and I made my choice. Not the choice she expected, but it was my choice.

I chose to stay.

I watch Emma as she runs away from us and stops next to a stall selling Christmas-themed gingerbread men coated in colorful icing. The woman behind the stall flashes Emma a wide smile, and they start discussing which one she would like to purchase with the dollars clutched in her small hand. Lily's attention is on her daughter, watching her like a hawk even though we're among trusted people.

"Never," I reply. "Or at least, not one like this. Fairs in the city are much more extravagant, but nothing like this. This is just… I have no words."

Snow falls gently onto an already white-coated town. The street is filled to the brim with wooden stalls and tents, all heaving with Christmas-themed items. From wooden figurines hand-carved by the local hunter to a stall covered in miniature snow globes that are so adorable, I almost want to purchase them all. They would look fantastic in my office. There's one stall selling homemade candles and scent sticks, one selling imported food from around the world, one selling knitted sweaters and woolly hats, and even one that has several hand-painted sleds on display.

There wouldn't be creativity like this back in the city. It really feels like the entire town has come together to showcase all their best pieces for the tourists who have come here for the perfect Christmas break, and for anyone else who needs a reminder of how great this little town is.

It's the most at home I have ever felt.

"You don't have a stall?" I ask as we lazily walk toward Emma.

"I do." Lily nods. "It's near the town square, but because there's a special edition of the Nativity tonight, I have my best friend running it so I can watch Emma. I've seen her perform three times already, but I want to see them all."

"Adorable," I say. I want to see it too. And then afterward, Lily and I need to talk. I'm firm in my choice to stay here, and ideally, I'd like that to include Lily and Emma if she will let me, but we still have a lot to talk about. I want to explain how naive I was when I returned to my family all those years ago and how I was certain we could maintain a long-distance relationship, but I had become so utterly swamped that time escaped me.

Then I was living a planned out life and Lily was just a dream.

But I want to change that. I want Lily to know exactly how I feel and in turn, I want her to share how she feels with me, too. But those words are hard, especially when it feels like saying anything will ruin this fantastic bubble we've found ourselves in.

"Look!" Emma laughs as she returns to us with a gingerbread clutched in her hand. "It looks like Amelia!"

Lily and I study the drooping icing face, which has so few features that it's a wonder it resembles anyone. Emma can clearly see something we miss.

"Yes." Lily chuckles uncertainly. "It really does. You will have to keep it and show it to her."

"Nah," Emma says, and she takes a large bite out of the head.

Lily laughs, and I slip my hand into hers. When she grips mine back, my heart soars and I feel untouchable. Even the cold that surrounds us feels kept at bay by the warmth radiating from my heart. We pass a few more stalls as we walk toward the town square where the final Nativity performance will be held. I spot Margret, who looks pointedly at my joined hand with Lily's and smiles.

I smile back. She will never know how integral she was in giving me the push toward reaching out to Lily. I never would have dared if I hadn't been forced into that corner of possibly losing my job. Now, I feel like I've truly earned my place.

People we pass call us a cute couple, and Emma runs into a few school friends who are just as excited about the show. Watching parents chat with Lily about school things, one question continues to worm in the back of my mind.

Mark isn't Emma's father, so who is? Why has Lily never mentioned him? Is he completely out of the picture? As I listen to Lily chat with other parents, I scan the crowds around us and every man I see becomes a possibility. I don't doubt Lily's secrecy, but if we are to pursue this, I want to know.

I adore her and Emma. I just need to know when her dad is going to sweep back into the picture.

Once we part with the parents, we run into Lily's parents who are hosting a stall and giving out mechanical advice and hot drinks for free. We all get hot chocolate, and Lily's mother gives me a very detailed rundown on what happens to car engines when the temperature gets below minus-thirty.

I tell myself I understand her but as we part ways, everything she said fades from my memory. I don't think I will ever understand cars.

The next stall we stop at is selling calendars and diaries. They're all adorable, and as Emma picks out one with Lily's supervision, I get my first talk about taking care of Lily.

It's the first of many as the night wears on. She's a well-loved figure in this town and there are several people all happy to tell me to make her happy, take care of her, or I'll answer to them. By the time we reach the homemade chili stall, it feels like half the town will hunt me down if I break her heart.

Luckily, I didn't know these people seven years ago. My response to each of them is the same. I have no desire to ever hurt Lily.

As Lily and Emma delve into small bowls of chili, I break away from the tables and head deeper into the market seeking out something I spotted on our walk over. Finding the stall, I make two purchases and hurry back to the meal area just as they finish their meal.

"Where were you?" Lily asks, licking her spoon. "Were you not hungry?"

"I was, but I realized I wanted to get these. Here." Sitting back down, I pull two handmade scarves out of my pocket and hand them each to

Lily and Emma. Lily gets a blue one covered in snowflakes and Emma gets a green one covered in snowmen.

"Oh, wow!" Emma gasps, messily throwing the scarf around her neck. "For me?"

"Yup."

"Oh, James." Lily is more delicate when putting her scarf on. "You didn't need to do this."

"I wanted to." I chuckle.

Emma suddenly launches herself into my arms and hugs me tightly. "Thank you, thank you!"

"Of course." I smile brightly, hugging her back, but I catch Lily watching us with a strange look on her face.

Emma pulls away, then sprints to the next table to show her friend her new scarf.

"Are you okay?" I ask Lily, trying to decipher the look on her face.

"I…" She shakes her head. "Did you mean it?" she asks. "Choosing to stay here over going back to your family?"

"Family isn't what they are. They're all rules and public opinion, and they've mapped out my life from birth to death. For the first time in my life, I feel like I'm really in control. I feel free. And that maybe life can surprise me now. It wasn't a hard decision at all. I think I'd already made it weeks ago and this was the final nail."

"Wow," Lily says softly. "You sound so different now when you talk. Like… like you're not weighed down anymore."

"It does feel like that," I reply, reaching for her hand. "Although there is something I've been wondering about."

"Mmmhmm?"

"You and me… we don't have to label it or anything, but I am having the time of my life with you. And I know that it might feel cheeky, given what happened between us all those years ago. It was so hard, getting swept up in family obligations, and by then, it was too late to reach out to you because you had surely moved on."

Lily frowns deeply. "Wait—"

"I just mean," I cut in hurriedly. "This makes me happy. I want to get to know you so much better. And Emma too. But I wonder about her father. Should I talk to him? Are there boundaries there that I should navigate?"

Lily's face pales slightly and she presses her lips together. "James, do you really—"

"Mommy!" Emma yells suddenly. "We're going to be late!"

Lily glances at her watch and then jumps up. "You're right! The show!" Lily and Emma rush off toward the square while I quickly pay for dinner and then head after them. They make it just in time, and Emma is whisked backstage. I find Lily in the crowd, but it's now too noisy for us to continue our conversation, although Lily looks faintly unwell.

The show begins and I watch, enthralled, as the children of the town act out the story of Christ. Emma is an adorable shepherd, although she loses her beard halfway through, much to the amusement of the crowd. Lily holds my hand through the entire thing.

We become slightly separated when the show is over and the crowd breaks up. As we head backstage, I find myself scanning the crowd, and my mind runs with the possibilities of what Lily is going to say.

Emma comes sprinting out of the small curtained changing area with a tinsel halo and throws herself into her mom's arms. "Did you see?" she yells. "Did you see me?"

Lily laughs. "I did."

Emma then wriggles free and charges toward me. I spot the melting ice cream bear in her hand just in time to avoid a sticky mess, and Emma latches on to me. "Did you see, Dad? Did you see?"

A slip of the tongue that punches me in the chest, and for a second, I can't breathe.

I glance up at Lily, and she's staring back at me, white as a sheet.

"Lily?" I ask softly, ruffling Emma's hair. "Lily, what's wrong?"

25

LILY

It was an innocent slip of the tongue. Emma didn't even notice she said it. But James did.

I did.

Hearing that word come from her was like getting punched in the gut, and my entire world shifted off-axis. James was worried, asking me if I was okay, and no matter how I tried to rearrange my face to hide how I was feeling, it didn't seem to work.

He kept a concerned eye on me for the rest of the night, even as we went to visit my parents so they could bury Emma in kisses because of her performance.

Is this happening?

Is my secret out?

For the rest of the night, everything around me seems slightly fuzzy. James sticks by my side, doing what he can to help, but each interaction he has with Emma just makes my heart ache more.

Does he suspect?

Does he know?

I can't tell. We head home, and I take Emma up to bathe. She plays in the bubbles while my mind loops on that single word. *Dad.* As I tuck her into bed, she asks if James will be here tomorrow so they can go ice skating again. I tell her I have no idea and read her a story until she falls asleep.

Back downstairs, James is waiting in the kitchen with a half-drunk bottle of wine and two glasses, one full and one empty.

As I enter, James refills the empty glass while sliding the other toward me. Without a word, I take the glass and head out onto the snow-covered patio, as if the cold will keep my emotions in check. And I don't want Emma to hear.

"Lily," James says as he joins me. "Do you want to tell me what's going on?"

"Not really," I sigh, wrapping my arms around myself and balancing the glass in my hand.

"Why did you look like you'd seen a ghost when Emma called me Dad? Is that what happened? Is her father dead?"

It would be easier that way, I think, if her father were some nameless person, a distant memory who didn't matter. Dead to me would be easier. But I can't keep this up. Sooner or later, James will learn the truth and it has to come from me.

He has to understand.

I sip my wine and stare out across the white garden, right to the edge where darkness swallows up the world.

"You haven't guessed?" I say softly.

"Guessed what?" James asks. He stands to my left, a few feet away, and I can't bring myself to face him. I don't want to see the pain on his face, or the anger.

"Emma's father. He's…" The words catch in my throat, and I close my eyes, hugging my glass to my chest. When I open them, James stands before me.

"Talk to me, Lily."

"He's you," I say hoarsely. "You are Emma's father."

All color drains from James's face. "What?"

"You are Emma's father."

He takes a half-step back. "Don't be ridiculous."

"Is it really so ridiculous? She's six years old, James. You never did the math when you saw her?"

His eyes dart back and forth. "But Mark… I thought…" His frown deepens as he trails off.

"I know. But you thought wrong."

"I don't understand." When James looks back up at me, there's anger in his eyes. "How could you keep this from me?"

My own hurt fades, replaced by the heat of my own anger. "You're joking, right?"

"No, I'm not fucking joking. How could you not tell me I had a *daughter*?"

"Because you didn't want to know!" I snap, taking my own step back toward the house. "You left me, James. Did you forget that tiny detail? Your father called you to heel and you just left. You went back to God knows where, back to your fancy family and fancy life, and you broke my heart!"

James's lips press into a thin line. "You *know* how hard my family are. I had no choice."

"You did! And you chose!"

"So what?" James snaps. "So what if I thought I did the right thing to keep my family happy? You had no right to keep my daughter from me."

"Don't you dare!" Heat builds behind my eyes and my heart races. "I tried everything. *Everything*. All I could think of was to get in touch with you because when I found out I was pregnant, I was so scared. I had no idea what to do. I didn't want to be that girl who came home from college with a baby, but that's what I was becoming. I thought I could at least come back with a man too."

"Then you didn't try hard enough!"

"No, James. You didn't. I was told that you didn't care, that you wanted nothing to do with me and there was nothing I could do to change that. After a bunch of rejections, I finally understood. You didn't *want* to be a father."

James begins to pace back and forth, wearing away the snow to the point that the wood gleams through. "No," he murmurs.

"Yes," I snap. "So I came home. I gave birth. I raised *my* daughter alone because you didn't care. And I understood after some time. You were going to be some rich, successful doctor and you didn't need me. In fact, you cared so little that you got your mother to tell me to back off!"

"My *mother*?"

"Yes! So don't you stand there and try to make me out to be the bad guy here. I did and have always done what is best for my daughter. She even tried to pay—"

"No. My mother would never. She has talked about grandchildren ever since I reached dating age!"

"You're not going to stand there and defend her after what I saw the other day. Are you serious?" My anger boils over and suddenly, nothing else matters. All I need is for James to understand how much he hurt me. "You *left* me, James. You didn't take my calls. You wanted nothing to do with me, so yes, I raised my daughter by myself."

"And us?" James yells back. "What, you were fucking me for old time's sake? Where does that factor in, huh? Did you not think that eventually, I'd start asking questions?"

"Doubtful," I mutter bitterly. "You thought Mark was the father, for fuck's sake. You clearly weren't working anything out."

"So you were never going to tell me?"

"I don't know! I hadn't planned on any of this. First it was a favor because I felt bad for you after your father, and then we started having fun, and I told myself it was only temporary, but now things are messy and confusing."

"I chose to stay here," James says tightly. "I chose to stay and you still didn't tell me."

"Because I was scared! The last time I tried to tell you, it was clear you were not—"

"Not true," James barks, and he points at me. "How do I know you didn't fail to try hard enough?"

"You think I wanted to be a single mother?" The glass nearly slips from my hand, so I slam it down onto the nearest snow-covered surface. "I *tried*. You were the one who never picked up. I had to speak to your mother!"

"And now?" James approaches me, his eyes dark. "Why wouldn't you tell me as soon as I turned up? Seven years of child support is overdue, wouldn't you say?"

"It was never about that," I snap heatedly. The anger itches along my skin, flushing hot repeatedly until I no longer feel the cold. "I didn't know if you were here to stay or if this was just some random stumble in your confidence. I wasn't going to disrupt Emma's life on the small chance that you could commit this time!"

"All this time, my child was right here and you—" James clenches his fist, raising it to his mouth. "How long would you wait before telling me? How long would I have to prove myself before you trusted me with the knowledge of my own child?"

"I don't know," I say, and I deflate slightly. "I hadn't thought that far because you've only been here a few weeks, and I guess I expected you to just leave again."

James halts his pacing and the anger in his eyes is suddenly replaced with open, honest hurt.

"I chose you," he says tightly. "And now you stand here, telling me you didn't even know if we had a chance at a future together? That after everything I have done and shown you, you don't trust me?"

My mouth falls open and my brain doesn't work. I can't think of anything to say, caught up in the frustration that suddenly, I'm the bad guy, but he was the one who left.

"I don't," I stammer. "I hadn't... I trust you, I just—"

"Yeah I get it," James snaps bitterly. "You didn't trust me with my own kid."

"I'm telling you now. Doesn't that mean something?"

"Only because you're forced to. You don't believe in me, do you?" James's voice drops low. "You don't believe we have a future together, do you?"

I have no answer. My tongue stumbles over too many thoughts so nothing comes out and James... this time, he doesn't wait.

He sets down his glass and strides past me into the house.

I hold it together until I hear the front door slam.

Then the tears come.

26

JAMES

How did it come to this?

I have a daughter. Emma. That adorable girl with the bright smile and the sharper knowledge about social media than I'll ever have, is my daughter.

It's a lot to take in, so after I leave Lily's place, I spend the next few hours just driving around the town. There isn't much to explore, so after circling the town seven or eight times, I drive to the edge of town and park near the ice skating rink.

Trying to make sense of everything Lily told me is almost impossible, along with the news that I am a father.

One thought makes me numb, while the other sends my mind racing at such speeds that I can't understand one thought before another ten end up on top. With the heater on full blast and my phone on silent, I stare out at the winter wonderland around me and then dig out the bottle of Scotch I'd purchased as a Christmas gift for Margret.

It calls to me. The cool bottle is a comforting weight in my hands, and

I trace the swirling patterns on the label with my eyes, repeating Lily's revelation over and over in my mind.

Emma is mine.

Lily fell pregnant seven years ago after we spent time together.

She claims she tried to reach out but was blocked at every turn. That trips me up because there is nothing my mother would love more than a grandchild. At every party she hosts, she spends hours talking in the ear of anyone who cares to listen about how important the family line is.

And underneath all the confusion as to whether Lily is telling the truth or if my mother had anything to do with this secret being kept from me, there's one thing that pains me more.

Lily didn't trust me.

She was happy to play families with me at the ice rink, the party, and the Christmas fair, but when it came to telling me the truth?

She did not trust that I would do right by my daughter.

By her.

And that hurts.

I stare at the bottle until my eyes mist over and then a sob crawls out of my heaving chest.

I cry.

I cry because I miss my father and he would be the man I would turn to for advice on how to parent. Some tears are a mix of joy and sorrow that I have a daughter and I have missed six years with her for reasons unknown. I cry because Lily didn't trust me, and part of me understands why.

The tears flow thick and fast, and on the side of a deserted road, surrounded by snow on the edge of town, I finally allow myself to feel all the turbulent grief I've been running from for the past six months.

I sob until I have no energy left, and then I drive back to the motel with the Scotch unopened in the passenger seat.

Sleep comes quickly that night from sheer exhaustion, and I leave town first thing in the morning.

I have to confront this face-to-face, and my mother is the only person who can give me the answers I need. Lily claims that she had been turned away multiple times, and I struggle to accept that truth because in my heart, I believe that a child would make all the difference.

If I'd known, if she'd reached out to me again, I would have come back in a heartbeat. Part of me always thought she had just moved on.

Surely, my mother wouldn't turn away her own grandchild?

It's not an answer I can get from Lily, though, so I fly back to New York City using my family name and an untouched credit card to find my mother in her penthouse.

When I enter, it's like walking into a time capsule as my father's belongings still litter the place.

She has her back to me, staring out over the city next to a gigantic silver Christmas tree covered in red decorations. It's thrice the size of her and yet she somehow still has more presence than it.

"Mom."

She spins to face me and a grin of delight spreads across her face when we lock eyes. The delicate glass in her hand is discarded on a nearby table, and she hurries over the expensive fur rug to reach me.

She never lets anyone walk on that rug.

"James!" She clutches at my arms and her long fingernails are like daggers in my biceps. "You came home! Oh, my goodness, this is wonderful! What a fantastic Christmas surprise! Oh, I can't wait to call your Aunt Eileen and tell her. She will be absolutely ecstatic!"

My patience is thin after such a long flight and no food, so I'm firm as I grab her by the shoulders and force her to take a step back.

"Mom. I came here because I need to ask you something."

"Of course, darling, anything!"

Glitter clings to her lashes, and her red-painted lips stretch eerily from ear to ear.

"Did you know I had a daughter?"

Her smile falters a fraction, and I instantly see the truth in her eyes. She tries to hide it with a fluttering of lashes and a strange, hollow laugh as she pats my arm.

"What? A daughter? Don't be silly!"

"Mom!" I tighten my grip a fraction. "This is serious. Did you know? Tell me the truth."

She laughs again, an awkward sound like wind escaping from a paper bag, then she jerks her shoulders free and clutches at the pendant around her neck. "Don't grab me like that, James. How dare you."

My heart begins to race faster and faster as she continues to dodge the question, leaving me with no choice but to raise my voice and press further.

"Lily!" I snap. "The woman whose house you barged into you. You've spoken to her before, haven't you? Tell me the truth, Mom, please." My voice cracks slightly as a tidal wave of upset creeps through my mind.

Mom doesn't meet my eyes.

"Alright, fine," she snaps like she's scolding a child. "Yes, I know your *tart* was pregnant."

My world narrows to a pinpoint and my heart pounds so hard that all I can hear is the blood rushing past my ears.

"But I did what any mother would do and I protected this family, do you hear me?" Mom points at me, and her smile is gone, replaced with the same grim face she wore when telling me my father had passed. "I protected this family. I protected you! Do you have any idea of the scandal if people found out you got a random working-class girl *pregnant?*"

The word curls past her lips with a note of disgust.

"We would never live it down, especially since she attended a college your father gave speeches to, *and* you weren't married!" Mom's fingers twisted more aggressively over her pendant. "And you never mentioned the silly girl, so I knew she wasn't pregnant."

Anger bursts through me like an explosion and I lash out at the nearest thing—a porcelain vase shatters against the wall, sending water, flower stems, and shards scattering all over the floor.

My mother squeals and stumbles backward.

"Why didn't you tell me?" I ask tightly, forcing each word out with a breath.

"Like I said, James. I was trying to protect you. I had no idea that she kept the child. Though, I suppose when she turned down the money, I should have suspected as much."

"Wait, what money?" The anger inside me fizzles through all of my muscles before settling heavily in my chest like a bowling ball. Breathing hurts. Swallowing hurts.

Mom moves away from me and back to the tree as the distant sounds of car horns and squealing brakes drift up from the city below.

"I offered her money, a lot of money, actually, if she got an abortion. That harlot refused so instead, I started making sure that she would never see a dime of our money. I was under the impression that she went ahead with the abortion and I thought that was the end of it." Mom adjusts a bauble on the tree, then she turns back to me with a smile on her face.

"You..." No wonder Lily didn't trust me. I can't fathom how scared she must have been to learn she was pregnant, only to end up with my mother trying to pay her to get rid of it.

"Did Dad know?" I ask hoarsely.

"No."

Suddenly, nothing else I could say to my mother even matters. I give her one last look and then turn around and stride toward the elevator.

"James? James! Where are you going?" She hurries after me, her high heels clacking loudly on the wooden floor. "James!"

"I only came here to hear the truth from you," I force out through the tension bleeding into my jaw. "And somehow, it's even worse than anything I ever could have imagined."

The elevator doors slide open, and I stride inside just as my mother reaches me. Tears sparkle in her eyes, and she clutches the door.

"Son, please. Stop and let's talk about this."

"No." There is nothing more to say. I can't even stomach looking at her anymore, so I avert my gaze to the floor. "Six years. I missed six years of my daughter's life because you—" I can't put the words together. "We are done, do you hear me? I will never speak to you again."

"James!"

Her wail echoes in the elevator as the doors close, and I'm swiftly sent down to the lobby. As I descend, I wonder how on earth I can make this up to Lily. Now that I know the truth, I have to do everything in my power to make it right.

AVA GRAY

I have to show her that I am here for her and Emma. I want to be in my daughter's life.

If she says no, I will show her that I will still always be here as a pillar of support.

Stepping out into the lobby, I'm striding toward the entrance when a familiar voice calls out to me.

"James?"

My shoes skid slightly on the marble floors as I turn. "Bernice?"

"I thought that was you!" My ex-fiancée, looking as glamorous as ever, hurries up to me with a bright, wide smile and a short, lanky man in tow. "I had no idea you were back in the city!"

"I'm not," I say as she quickly pulls me into a brief hug. As she steps back, I spot that she's hand in hand with the man. "It was just a fleeting visit."

"To see your mother?" Sympathy bleeds into her tone. "You'd think I'd personally poured pig blood over her furs, the way she keeps calling my mother."

"I'm sorry." I chuckle. "But yeah, I had something I needed to straighten out with her."

"Are you staying for Christmas? A few of us are going to have Christmas Eve drinks at Lacey's if you want to join us?" Bernice's smile is so happy and hopeful, nothing like it was when we were together. She must be really happy now.

"I can't. I have somewhere I need to be. And I'm sorry, I'm James." I offer my hand to the smiling, silent man at Bernice's side, and he grips it firmly.

"Adam."

"The barista, right?"

His cheeks dust pink as he nods, and Bernice giggles, turning to peck him on the cheek.

"I'm sorry," she says. "Yes, this is the barista I'm sure you've heard so much about."

"Honestly, I don't pay attention anymore," I assure her, then I look back at Adam. "It's nice to meet you, man. You both look really happy."

"We are." Adam nods, and he looks at Bernice with such admiration that my heart swells and Lily floods my mind.

"I'm glad. Anyway, I have to go. Merry Christmas!" As I turn to leave, Bernice catches my elbow lightly.

"James, wait. If you're not staying for Christmas, then where are you going?"

I flash her the strongest smile I can muster. "I'm going home to win my family back."

27

LILY

James left.

I don't know why I expected anything different. The morning after our fight, my parents called to say that James had left really early and they thought they were giving me a heads up to an early surprise.

Instead, James was seen leaving town and that was that.

Deep down, I knew this would happen, but proving myself right just came with a bucket load of tears and crushing disappointment. I had fallen for him all over again and now, just like I feared, he learned of his fatherhood and he took off, likely on the first plane back to New York.

The only thing that made it worse was when Emma came down for breakfast and immediately asked where James was. I tried to tell her that he'd been called away, but she'd babbled on and on about how she hoped he would be back by Christmas so he could see her dance and they could go ice skating together.

At first, I tried to appease her, but it simply became too painful. After one too many cheery declarations that we had to get extra Christmas dinner for James, I snapped at her and told her the truth.

He didn't like us anymore and he was never coming back.

That word choice was harsh for a six-year-old, and I spent all afternoon apologizing and drying my daughter's tears. But the damage was done.

I had let James back into my life when I should have kept that door firmly closed.

Now I'm heartbroken again, and I have a six-year-old with no clue that her father has just walked out on her. Again.

By the time I get her down to sleep, I'm utterly exhausted and it had completely slipped my mind that Amelia is coming over to help with presents until she turns up at my door with sparkling wine and paper.

"Surprise! Oh, Lily." Amelia sobers up the moment she clocks my tear-filled eyes and streaked face. "Oh, sweetie."

I have no words as I wave her inside and trudge toward the kitchen in search of glasses.

"Do you want to tell me what happened?" Amelia asks while unwinding the scarf from her neck. "Or do you just want a sounding board so you can shit talk him?"

Collecting glasses from the top shelf, I sigh deeply and set them down next to the wine bottle, then I dab at my leaking eyes.

"There's not much to say." I sniffle. "He was starting to work things out. Emma was getting close to him. I was too, so I just opened my big mouth and told him the truth."

Amelia shakes snow from her hair, picks up her glass, and then follows me into the lounge.

"And?" she asks, kneeling down on the floor. "What did he say?"

AVA GRAY

I roll my eyes with a soft groan. "He said he had no idea that I'd tried to reach out, and he got defensive over his mother, and then he was hurt that I didn't trust him with the truth."

"Oh, wow." Amelia sips her drink as she nods. "And then he left?"

"For good." I wince. "My parents saw him pack up and leave the in. He's gone, Amelia. Really gone."

Hot tears well up behind my lids, and I whimper, then sink into her outstretched arm. For a few long moments, there are no sounds but my muffled sobbing and the soft, gushing sounds rumbling around Amelia's throat. She holds me tight, and I bury into her knitted sweater until the wave of tears passes.

"Anyway." I sniffle thickly and seek out some tissues. "Now Emma keeps asking about her friend, so I snapped at her and she cried, and I cried, and now I have no clue what to do because yesterday, I thought I was heading toward a fairytale Christmas and today, I'm just…" I stare dejectedly at the Santa Christmas paper Amelia brought with her. "Today, I feel like all the joy has been sucked right out of me."

"You really fell for him again, huh?" Amelia murmurs, cupping my damp cheek. "I'm sorry. I was so happy for you, and seeing the way he looked at you, I was sure this time would be different. He really seemed like he wanted a future here."

"I guess he did until he learned he would have to be responsible for a child," I reply, my heart heavy with dejection. "It's like his desire just shriveled up. He was so angry, too. Like I was the bad guy for keeping this a secret."

Amelia watches me closely and her lips part as if she's about to change her mind, then she shakes her head. "Where are the pressies?"

"Under the stairs," I say, pointing behind me and through the door to the cupboard under the stairs. "But what was that look?"

Amelia stands and hurries through to the hall. "What look?"

"That look. The look you just gave me that's like sad and not sad all at the same time." I gulp my wine down while waiting for Amelia to return with the presents, and when she does I refill my glass.

"There was no look."

"There was a look," I insist. "Go on, say whatever you were going to say."

Amelia sighs, crossing her legs as she settles beside me on the floor and picks up the scissors to cut the paper.

"Look. I'm with you on this, Lily. A thousand percent. And I'm not trying to justify anything because if you want to curse him out, then that is what we will do. But…"

"But?" I demand.

"From his perspective, he did just learn that not only did the woman he likes have his kid, but he also missed six years of his daughter growing up and apparently had no clue that you were ever pregnant. The dude probably just had the shock of his lifetime that you tried to reach out to him."

"And his answer is to leave?"

"Given that he ran away when his father died, I'd take a guess that he needs space to process huge news like this." Amelia smiles warmly and clasps my knee. "Like I said, I'm not justifying what he did. But maybe it wouldn't hurt to give him a little time to work through things."

"I didn't want that, though." I look over at my friend. "I wanted him to tell me that he was sorry for leaving. That he wanted to be right here with me and Emma. I wanted him to promise that he wouldn't leave and that he wanted us to be a family."

"I know, honey, I know."

"Does that make me a terrible person? Part of me is telling myself that I shouldn't be upset because I saw this coming and I knew he would leave because why would time change anything?" The tears well again, and I clutch at one of the stuffed animals I purchased for Emma's Christmas. "And then the other part of me yearns for him to be here so that I can give Emma the family she deserves."

"Okay, well for starters, you are all the family Emma needs, okay? You and your mom and dad. You do a fantastic job, okay? And second, you're not wrong for wanting those things. By all accounts, everything was going good, right? I don't think there's anything wrong with hoping that you can get the fairytale ending."

"Mmhmm." I nod along to Amelia's words, fighting to keep the tears at bay.

"You couldn't anticipate how he would react. That's not on you. You did what you thought was best for you and Emma, and no one can fault you for that. Certainly not him." Amelia gently tosses a strand of green ribbon toward me. "Don't beat yourself up, okay? Be sad, sure, but don't punish yourself."

If only it were that easy to follow her advice. We settle into an amicable silence with an old Christmas movie on the TV and the bottle of wine rapidly draining while we wrap presents.

Emma's are secured first just in case she decides to come hurrying down those stairs and walk in on us. Once they're out of the way, I wrap up the presents I have for my parents and Amelia uncorks the second bottle of wine.

Alcohol makes the tears come faster, but it's somewhat therapeutic to cry it all out with my best friend, even if we are surrounded by festive things for the supposed happiest day of the year. Amelia talks about work and her plans to go visit her parents next year while also gleefully informing me that Mark was fired and will be nowhere near me or my daughter ever again.

By the time the second bottle is empty, there's a nice stack of presents around the tree and my heart isn't as heavy as it was a few hours ago.

Amelia and I lounge next to each other, watching the next Christmas movie through a haze of alcohol.

"You know," Amelia says suddenly, "you should come out with me for my work Christmas night out on Christmas Eve."

"And get absolutely hammered?"

"No," Amelia scoffs. "Although that would be funny. Just come out with us, have a nice meal, and do something really fun. Take your mind off things and destress before the big day. Let me cheer you up properly and you can see that Christmas can still be joyful?"

"I'm in Grinch mode now," I mutter, tilting my empty wine glass around my leg. "Won't I be intruding?"

"Lily, I'm asking you to come. No one will care. We can have a really girly night and you can forget all about Mr. Tall, dark, and handsome. At least for one night."

"Hmm. Okay, sure. But only if I can get a babysitter."

"Excellent!" Amelia stands, wobbling slightly, and gathers up the empty bottle, then she moves off to the kitchen.

In her absence, I pull out my phone and study James's contact. He's called me once but I didn't pick up because I was too scared, and then he never called back. I haven't texted him either because I honestly don't know what to say.

I don't know if any excuse he can provide will be good enough... unless he's just calling to organize child support, in which case I don't want his money.

But I will take it for Emma.

"Don't tell me you are drunk dialing." Amelia snorts as she returns with a third bottle of wine.

"No, I'm just... I don't know. It doesn't feel serious right now."

"That's because you are drunk, darling."

"I'll regret this in the morning," I say, and yet I don't tilt my glass away as Amelia refills it.

As she settles next to me to finish out the rest of the film, the alcohol doesn't keep *all* the pain at bay.

Simmering underneath the fuzzy warmth of distance is the single thought that I missed out.

"Here's to being alone at Christmas," I say sadly, raising my glass. Amelia knocks our drinks together and cheers.

The happy family on the screen is picture-perfect happiness, and I so badly wanted that for Emma and me.

Instead, I fucked that up spectacularly.

28

JAMES

I have a plan.

It might be a terrible plan, but it's the only plan I have.

After the revelation from my mother that she tried to pay Lily to have an abortion, my perspective switched on the entire situation. It now made so much sense to me why Lily was so cagey about the whole thing. She was probably doing everything she could to protect herself and her daughter from any further harm that came from me or my family, and I can't say I blame her.

With three days to go until Christmas, I know I have to go big. It's my only option, my only chance to prove to Lily how I feel and that I want to spend the rest of my life with her and Emma. Then she will be free to make her own choice and I will respect it.

Returning to Evergreen Falls, my first stop is the inn, where I quickly speak to Lily's parents and lay out the details of my plan. Her mother has some choice words for me at first, but I don't blame her, considering how things looked when I left. After some apologies and promises, they agree to help me on one condition—that I keep Lily's best interests in my heart.

That is the easiest promise to make.

Next, I visit several stores around town searching for the perfect gift. I want to find something meaningful that Lily can hold on to as a symbol of my commitment. I get the same look at each store I go into. News travels faster than a fever in this town, so to all, I am the one who broke Lily's heart.

I accept those looks, and to a few trusted individuals, I reveal my plan. They grow just as excited as I am and are eager to offer their assistance in setting up what would be the grand setting for my idea. I graciously accept all help—paid, of course—and very quickly, my idea is becoming a reality.

The hardest thing about being back in town, however, is avoiding Sweet Noel. Part of me yearns to kick down that door and sweep Lily away so I can explain everything to her, but I resist. I have to do this right. I have to show Lily exactly what she means to me.

So I resist.

In between dodging calls from my mother and then my aunt once I block my mother's number, I also have to field calls from Margret, who is furious that I just disappeared one morning and left the clinic in the lurch for two days.

Upon stepping into her office, she yells at me for a solid eighteen minutes before taking a breath and letting me speak. I am honest with her because she has always been good to me, and I explain the true cruelty my mother had inflicted on Lily, as well as my part in dealing with the revelation poorly.

Margret smacks me on the shoulder and orders me to make it up to Lily, and I am more than happy to inform her that I plan to do exactly that. I just need a little bit of time.

Once Margret learns the secret, naturally, everyone else knows, and I have to trust that no one will reveal things to Lily until the right moment. This leads me to her best friend, Amelia.

Amelia is the only one not swayed by my romantic plan because, like me, she has Lily's best interests at heart, and I am the bad guy. She does listen to me, though, standing behind her desk brandishing scissors that I'm sure she wants to stab into my neck, and then she agrees to play the most crucial part.

All I need is for Amelia to get Lily to a certain place by a certain time, and then the rest will be up to fate. Will Lily accept me and listen to what I have to say? Or will she turn me away and become nothing more than a distant love while I work hard to support the daughter I missed?

The night before Christmas Eve, I sit in my inn room and pore over the Sweet Noel website. A new accolade has been added to celebrate the success of the auction, and Lily is making herself available to other charity events. I scroll until I reach the bottom where there is a picture of Lily hugging Emma, and my heart clenches.

Now that I know the truth, it's hard to understand how I missed the resemblance. Emma looks a lot like me, and that should warm me, but I don't allow myself to accept those feelings—not yet.

What happens next is not about what I want. It's about Lily and what she's had to deal with ever since I left her all those years ago. I can say what's in my heart and make a thousand promises, but at the end of the day, Lily is the one who knows what is best for her and Emma.

I tell myself that I will accept her decision no matter what, but even as night falls and a blanket of stars drapes across the town, visible from my window, my heart yearns for more.

The pain of living without Lily but being in Emma's life will be enough for me. And if they want me to keep their distance, I can do that too.

I lie back and stare through the curtains to the stars above, absently counting them as I run through what it felt like to see Lily again after so long. She pushed back the tidal wave I was drowning under and went out of her way to help me.

I'm now more certain than ever that I never stopped loving her. I just buried it deep because I thought that was the right thing to do.

I now know that I should have followed those feelings. I might be too late in doing it now, but it's all I have left to offer.

As I close my eyes, I fantasize about Lily running into my arms and kissing me with such passion that I can't hold back my tears. Then I envision Emma joining us and her sweet voice calling me *Dad* over and over again.

Those thoughts carry me into restless sleep with only one last thought on my mind.

Tomorrow, I may wake up to a reality in which Lily wants nothing to do with anyone from the Anderson family ever again.

I have one chance to change her mind.

29

LILY

"You're really not going to tell me where we're going?"

It's Christmas Eve and Amelia turned up at my house with a bright smile, insisting that I dress up. I'd agreed to attend her work Christmas night out a few days ago, but I'd been under the impression that it would be just me, her, and a few friends.

Suddenly, I needed to bring Emma.

"Nope," Amelia says as she walks beside me, popping the *P* with a grin. "I just need you to trust me."

"You know I can't take Emma into the bar, right?" I remind her.

Amelia nods and glances past me at Emma. She's stomping through the mounds of snow lining the sidewalk with her small, gloved hand clutched in my own. A bitterly cold wind dances past us, kicking up loose snow and sending it swirling into the air.

Walking through town on Christmas Eve is a magical experience. Every shop has its lights on, and a variety of twinkling colors spills from decorated windows onto the snow-covered ground. People hurry past us, caught up in their last-minute Christmas shopping, and I don't envy them. To some, it's almost a tradition.

And yet, as I watch people huddle together hand in hand against the cold, the sadness that's swamped me these past two days threatens to rise up once more. I still haven't had the confidence to reach out to James, deciding instead to have a nice Christmas with my family and then I'll tackle all of that in the New Year.

James hasn't reached out to me either, so I'm not even confident there will be anything to reach out to.

"Where are we going?" Emma whines, stomping her pink boots more aggressively into the snow. "I'm cold!"

"I know, sweetie," I soothe her. "But Amelia has a surprise for us. And then I'll take you to Grandma's and we can set up the tree, okay?"

Every year for as long as I can remember, my parents have refused to decorate their own Christmas tree until Christmas Eve. Our family tradition is that all other decorations will be set up to make the place look festive, but the tree will always be last. I'm fairly certain it's because my mother's work used to take her out of town, but she would always be back by Christmas Eve, and thus, one of our favorite traditions was born.

"Not much farther," Amelia assures me as we cross the street toward the town square. "I just need you both to promise me one thing."

"Both of us?" I ask curiously, wondering if Amelia is leading us to the ice skating rink. If she is, I wish we'd taken the car.

"Both of you."

"Okay!" Emma grins and her rosy-red nose scrunches up as she sniffles.

"Remember that I love you," Amelia says, and she locks eyes with me. "And that I support you no matter what."

The uncertainty in my chest grows heavy, and I frown at Amelia. "What do you mean? You're kind of starting to worry me."

"Trust me," is all Amelia says, and she takes my hand, squeezing gently. "Okay?"

"Okay." I nod, and yet the uncertainty still swarms my gut like a flutter of heavy-winged butterflies. Emma is clueless and resumes her attempts to place a boot print on every untouched patch of snow, few as they are.

I have more to ask Amelia, but suddenly, she speeds up her walking, and distance forms between us. She doesn't stop until she reaches the crosswalk, and then she turns to me with the widest smile on her face.

"I love you, Lily. You know that, right?" she says.

"Of course I do. I love you too. Amelia, what is it because you're..."

My words die in my throat as I reach the crosswalk and the Town Square becomes visible.

It's been beautiful since the day everyone came together and started decorating it, but something is different.

A warm orange glow rises from all of the shops and buildings surrounding the square, creating an oval of amber light that sweeps across the town square and frames the central gazebo. The gazebo is covered in white lights that subtly flash and pulse in time to soft, classical music drifting through the air.

Every tree is covered in blue, red, and green lights that reflect off the silver tinsel winding across the branches. Several fake snowmen are covered in glitter that makes them sparkle with the slightest movement from me. The scents of chocolate, ginger, and cinnamon fill the air, and I'm distantly aware that there are no people around, which is strange for this time of night.

But all of that pales in comparison to what is in the middle of the town square.

A long string of new golden lights stretches from one tree to another, twinkling in the darkness like a scattering of stars fell from the heavens and lined up just for me.

"Look, Mommy!" Emma gasps, pointing at the lights. Her eyes are so wide that they reflect the sparkles, and my heart begins to race. The lights above are carefully arranged to spell out a phrase I never could have imagined.

Will you be my family?

Below the lights, looking incredibly nervous while holding a single rose, stands James.

"It's James!" Before I can stop her, Emma twists out of my grip and sprints across the crosswalk toward the town square. She runs until she crashes headlong into James, who ducks to catch her with a laugh.

James is here.

He's *here*.

Part of me honestly thought I would never see him again, yet he stands there like something out of a dream and I have no idea what to say. A hand presses gently into the small of my back, urging me forward, and I obey because I have no idea what else to do.

All I can think about is our last argument and the heartbreaking realization that he was abandoning me once again. Yet here he stands.

As I get closer, I can decipher the hopeful look in his eyes. When I reach the snow-covered grass in front of him, he smiles shakily and begins to speak.

"Lily. I know I have no right to ask this but please, give me two minutes to say what I want to say and then, whatever you want to do after that, I will do it."

Emma skips back to me with the biggest grin on her face, so I nod because I don't trust myself to speak. A commotion of emotions clashes together inside me—anger that he left and then didn't talk to me for two days, hurt that he didn't believe me about his mother, hope that seeing him again could mean he wants to stay, and confusion at the lights.

What the hell is going on?

"I am so deeply sorry for walking out the other night. I have no excuse other than I was completely stunned by what you told me, and it didn't fit with what I knew at the time. It doesn't excuse what I did, but I hope it helps you understand why I had to get away."

As he talks, clouds of condensation curl past his lips and spiral up to the sparkling lights above.

"I went back to the city and confronted my mother. I needed to hear it from her directly because Lily, you have to believe me. I had *no* idea that you were pregnant, or that you even tried to reach out. I thought we had gone our separate ways and I wanted to respect that. But my mother finally told me the truth."

His jaw twitches, and my heart continues to race like a rabbit trapped within a cage.

"She hid it from me for the good of the *family*, in her words. She also told me that she tried to pay you and, Lily, I am so sorry you had to go through that alone."

Hearing it come from James's mouth is strange because that secret—that his mother offered me money for an abortion—has never been uttered out loud. I kept that hidden within me as the main fuel to never look for James or his family again. Hearing that he was completely in the dark stuns me.

Should I have tried harder to reach him? Could things have been different?

Tears sparkle in James's eyes as he steps forward. "I love you, Lily," he says softly. "I loved you seven years ago and I never stopped. I squashed it down because I was fighting to make other people happy, but I am done with that life. I am done pretending to be someone I'm not and hiding how I feel. I love you so much, Lily. Some days, it consumes me. I look at you and everything in the world is brighter, and it's like I can finally see color for the first time. I think about you all the time, and I have ever since I first saw you in your bakery. I love you."

My warring emotions surge upward, battling for dominance, but there's a clear winner. My anger fades. I met his mother, and I can't blame him for not taking action when he had no idea that I was trying to reach him. And Amelia was right—James needed time to process and confront the truth. Which means he believed me enough to fly back to the city and hear it from the horse's mouth.

Pressure swells in my chest, and I try to speak, but all I do is gasp as a stray tear leaks down my cheek.

"So I'm here, Lily. For you. And Emma. I want to be a good man for you, Lily. I want to make you proud and make you feel happy and safe. I want to be a good father for Emma. If I had known all those years ago, I would have been here in a heartbeat, I *swear* it."

Emma's hand suddenly grips mine, and when I glance at her, she stares up at me with glassy eyes. "My dad?" she asks with a croak.

My heart breaks apart at the look of pure hope on her face. Her view is innocent, and the stories I've told her about her absent father have never created any anger in her. She's looking at me for answers.

"Oh, and..." James suddenly comes a lot closer and he holds out his hand to me. In his palm sits a pair of hand-crafted, wooden, carved ice skates. One has my name and the other has Emma's name. "When we went ice skating, that was the day I realized that everything I had ever wanted in life was right here, with you and Emma. So these, if you accept them, are a symbol of our past and present coming together. And hopefully, our future."

He chokes up slightly and his hand trembles, his fingertips turning pink from the cold.

"Mommy?" Emma asks again, and we lock eyes.

I can't lie to her. I can't do it, not now. "Yes," I say, finally finding my voice. "Yes, he is your father."

"Daddy!" Emma squeals and launches herself forward, tackling James's leg with such force that he stumbles backward. Reflex has me reaching out for his hand to help him maintain his balance, and our hands close over the wooden trinkets.

"You took so long to come home!" Emma wails, and the dam breaks as she sobs against his leg. There's a flash of confusion across James's face as he crouches down to comfort her, then he pulls her in for a tight hug as tears fall down his own cheeks.

"I know," he said hoarsely. "I know. I'm sorry. But no matter what, I'm here, okay? And I'll always be here."

A trembling sob escapes me, and I place one hand over my mouth, searching for the right thing to say. Maybe there isn't a right thing to say. When James stands, he offers me the rose that is now slightly crumpled after being caught in the hug between him and Emma.

"So," he whispers. "What do you say?"

"You left," I croak. "You left and I had no idea if you were coming back. I thought you hated me, that I had made a mistake."

"No," James says. "I was the one who made the mistake. Blinded by my mother and her laws for too long. I love you, Lily, and if you accept me, I will spend every day for the rest of my life making up for it."

My heart swells bigger and bigger, pressing against my ribcage and limiting my breaths from how overwhelmed I feel.

There is only one answer, but I have to make sure.

"If you're here," I say shakily, "then you have to *be* here. You can't leave just because things get hard. Do you understand? She knows now." I glance down at Emma. "Which means you have to be *here*."

"I'm here," he says, and another tear escapes down his handsome face. "I only left to get answers. This is where I want to be, Lily. I love you. I want this. I want you and our family. But only if you want that too."

I must be dreaming. Gigantic flakes of snow begin to drift slowly down around us, sharply kissing my cheeks where they land. Staring into James's eyes, I'm even more convinced this is some kind of dream.

"Yes," I say, and all my overwhelming emotions bubble forward as I sob. "Yes, I love you too. I do, I love you too!"

James sweeps me into his arms, and his lips crash against mine in a heated, biting kiss. Our tears mingle, and the taste of salt invades the kiss, but I don't care. His arms are around me, our daughter is clinging to our legs, and my heart soars to be caught up in his hold.

Suddenly, soft cheers and clapping rise up from around me and we break apart with a laugh. On the other side of the street, several of the townsfolk have emerged from their stores and are cheering us on, led by Amelia who is dabbing at her own eyes.

"I had a little help to set this up," James whispers in my ear, repeatedly kissing my cheek.

Overwhelming love pours through me, and I cup James's cheek, kissing him deeply once more.

Christmas really is the perfect time of year.

30

JAMES

"Merry Christmas." Lily's hands slide around my waist and press flat against my abdomen. Her grip tightens, and she draws me back against herself, pulling my attention away from the dessert I was very carefully placing sugar candy stars onto.

Christmas Day has been magical from start to finish. I woke early, still unable to believe that Lily had said yes to the question, and showered quickly. By the time I headed downstairs, the inn was filled with light and music as Lily's parents hosted a Christmas breakfast for all the guests still staying there, myself included. Lily and Emma arrived a little after ten, and I had the privilege of watching Emma open up all of her gifts.

I took note of everything she was given, cataloging it in my mind as things she liked. I was over the moon that she loved my gift of the snow globe I'd seen her eyeing at the Christmas fair last week. Lily was quick to place the snow globe someplace safe, but Emma was happy, and thus, so was I.

I know there are harder conversations to come about childcare and the like, but right now, everyone is embracing the Christmas spirit, and I'm not going to change that.

"You've been in here all afternoon," Lily murmurs, ending the hug by stepping away and leaning on the counter next to me. "Are you hiding?"

"Who would I be hiding from?" I ask softly. "I'm helping."

"Well, helping my parents prepare dinner is a really sweet gesture, but you are allowed to come out of here every so often."

I place another few stars, then turn to Lily with a warm smile. "Trust me, I'm having a blast. I can't even really explain how amazing it is to have a home-cooked meal at Christmas, or even how great it is to help and have a hand in it."

"I take it your mother isn't a cook?" Lily scoffs, swiping one of the sugar stars and popping it into her mouth.

"Not even a little. Everything was catered or purchased in some way. Seeing everything you do with your family, even since I got here, has been amazing. So trust me." I lean forward and lightly kiss the tip of her nose. "I am not hiding. I'm enjoying things."

"Are you sure you're not scared of my mother?" Lily laughs.

"I mean, a little. When I told her about what I wanted to do for you at the town square, I thought she was going to clock me with a wrench and send me right back to the city," I say softly. "I was *very* aware of how people adore you in this town, and getting them on board was probably the scariest thing."

"Oh, really?" Lily steals another sugar star.

"Other than facing you and pouring my heart out," I add. "That was pretty damn scary."

"I'm glad you did." Lily turns those gorgeous eyes to me. "I'm not saying everything is magically fixed, but I think we have a good start. Plus, it's Christmas."

The next time she tries to steal a sugar star, I catch her wrist and pull her toward me. Lily comes easily with a cheeky smile, and I lean into her, making her curve backward slightly. The warmth of the kitchen creates a rosy flush across her cheeks, and her eyes dart over my face as I lean closer.

"If you eat all of those, there's none for the pudding."

"Shame." She giggles. "Should keep a better eye on them, then."

"Because *that's* my issue," I murmur, bringing my lips within a hair's breadth of hers. "And not your sticky fingers."

"Mmmhmm." Lily grins, cupping my cheek with her soft hand. Her thumb skims across my jaw, then she closes the gap and presses a slow, lingering kiss to my lips. It's just a single kiss and yet my heart immediately begins to race and a different heat flushes down my body.

As she pulls away, I chase her lips and kiss her deeply with a soft groan. Her hands slide around my neck, and she toys with my hairline while my tongue teases across the seam of her lips.

There's no telling where we'd stop if not for the egg timer suddenly trilling loudly, and we both pause.

"Your pudding?" Lily asks with a smirk.

"Your dad's pastry, actually," I correct softly, pecking her lips once more.

We straighten up, and Lily slides away, snagging a few more sugar stars on her way out. "Just don't stay in here forever."

I spend the next hour in the kitchen, joined eventually by Lily's mother and father. I can't express how much it means to me that they let me be a part of this, and helping cook lifts my spirits higher than I'd ever imagined.

By the time we sit down for Christmas dinner, I'm mostly giddy. Lily sits next to me and Emma sits one chair down, but she babbles to me as if we are right beside one another. Lily's father carves the chicken, and I dish out the greens and potatoes that I helped with, while Emma's mother is in charge of the sauce, the sprouts, and all the trimmings.

It's not the most extravagant Christmas meal I've ever eaten, but it immediately becomes my favorite. Sitting around a rickety wooden table that creaks every time someone moves a plate, dressed in Christmas sweaters with musical carols playing in the air... it's heaven. We eat, laugh, and joke about the year. Emma's mother talks about some expansion details she has for next year, while her father mentions a desire to return to his old hobby of crochet.

More things I store in my mind as I learn about these people.

Then it's time for dessert. I serve the dish I made with a proud grin, and when serving Lily's slice, I scatter a few extra sugar stars on her plate.

Then Emma speaks up and brings the entire table to silence.

"Daddy?"

The word still sounds strange, and I pause in serving, feeling as if Emma has just punched me right in the center of my chest. I don't think I will ever tire of hearing that term. Everyone else goes silent, and I hover over the table, unsure what to do.

Lily's mom stands and takes the serving spoon from me. Then she flashes me an encouraging smile and nods toward Emma.

I sit slowly and face my daughter. "Yes?"

"Can you come to the dance with me?"

My heart pounds so hard, it's a wonder no one else at the table can hear it. I want to say yes. I want to run outside and scream in delight that my daughter, such a new addition to my life, already wants me to attend the daddy/daughter dance with her.

I look to Lily's father who seems completely unfazed by the question, but the last thing I want to do is step on his toes when Emma has a tradition of asking him.

Lily's hand moves to my thigh and her lips part, but before she can speak, her father talks instead.

"I think that's a swell idea," he says in between mouthfuls of pudding. "My hip has been playing up, so I couldn't dance even if I wanted to."

He's giving me his blessing in a way that's subtle, and yet it means so much. The static sting of emotion rises behind my eyes, and I swallow audibly, then look at Emma.

"I would *love* to," I say, fighting to keep my voice strong. "It would be my honor."

"Yay!" Emma is oblivious to my emotional turmoil, but Lily sees it all and she keeps her hand on my leg for the remainder of the meal.

So much of this still doesn't feel real.

After dinner, we all bundle up into our winter coats and head out to the town hall where the daddy/daughter dance is being held. Lily and I walk with Emma singing and jumping around between us, and she's a ball of energy until we reach the hall. Then she becomes subdued and as we head toward the dance hall, she begins to lag behind.

Her grandparents go on ahead while Lily and I take Emma off to the side.

"Are you okay, sweetie?" Lily asks, kneeling in front of Emma. "Do you want to go home?"

Emma shakes her head.

"Do you want to change your dress?"

Again she shakes her head. Lily sighs softly, then her head tilts. "Is it because of what your classmates were saying?"

Emma nods.

"What did they say?" I ask softly, confusion swirling in my chest. "Is something wrong?"

"Just childish bullies," Lily murmurs as she stands back up. "They've been teasing Emma because she's been bringing her grandpa to these dances."

Oh.

Kids are assholes.

I lower down to my haunches in front of Emma and hold out my hand. "You know, it doesn't matter what they say but I can promise you, if we walk out there right now, they won't be able to say anything because we are going to be the best dancers out of everyone."

Emma's eyes light up and then she finally takes my hand. "Do you know the chicken?" she asks.

I glance at Lily, who merely laughs, and then I shake my head. "I don't know the chicken."

Emma rolls her eyes in a way that reminds me of Lily and drags me forward. We spend the next ten minutes learning the chicken dance, and then it's showtime.

I don't notice the decorations or the other parents filing into the hall. I don't pay attention to the other children, the catering table, or even Lily in the stands.

For the entire dance, my sole focus is on Emma. We dance around the room together, sometimes in sync but mostly out of sync. Not that it matters. The smile on her face is delightful and it quells all the uncertainty in my heart. I have a lot to make up for concerning Emma and Lily, but this is a beautiful place to start.

I'll take her to these dances until I'm eighty just to see her smile like this, and even if she decides she no longer wants to, I will remember this forever. We dance for what feels like hours until Emma's heartwarming smiles and laughter melt into yawns and swaying. After our final loop of the dance hall, I scoop her up into my arms, and she nuzzles in as I carry her back to where Lily sits with her parents.

"Aww, look at her," Lily coos. "She's all tuckered out."

"She's not the only one," I say as I pass Emma into Lily's arms, then lightly kiss Lily's cheek. "She was out almost as soon as I picked her up."

As a group, we leave the hall, and as we head down the hallway toward the outer doors, Lily's father holds out one hand to me.

I accept it with a flicker of a frown.

"It's about time we saw this family complete," he says with a smile, clasping my shoulders.

His words, and the warmth in his eyes, catch me by surprise. That may just be the most affection I've ever received from a parental person, and the fact that he really seems to mean it affects me more than I can say.

My heart clenches painfully at the absence of my own father, and I realize that with Lily accepting me into her life, I'm gaining more than just a girlfriend and a daughter. I'm gaining a full family.

"Thanks for having me," I say as we step outside and come to a stop, Lily and her mother taking in the beautiful scene before us.

The entire parking lot is covered in thick snow, and fat snowflakes drift down from the sky. With the sparkling Christmas trees near the entrance, a swell of festive spirit surges through me and I place my arm around Lily's waist.

"Merry Christmas."

31

LILY

The days after Christmas come with a warmth they've never had before. Partly, it comes from having James around the house. He settles in immediately and does everything he can to help, and even though it's only been a few days, I find myself incredibly grateful for him.

For the first time in six years, I'm able to take a bath undisturbed and sleep in. Emma wants to spend all her time with James, and I can't blame her. We did sit her down and explain everything to her, as much as we could explain to a six-year-old, at least, and while she showed signs of confusion, she was mainly just happy to have James here and with us.

Questions will likely come later.

That strange week between Christmas and New Year's when nothing feels real is made all the more dreamy by James's determination to treat us at every turn. He lavishes us in gifts and affection, and I can tell he's desperately trying to make up for his reaction and his absence. I don't have the heart to put my foot down yet, though, and watching Emma have one of her best Christmases ever is the cherry on top.

A couple of days after the dance, Emma leaves with her grandparents to go ice skating, which gives me the time I need to start packing up some of the Christmas clutter that's invading my home. I trash all the Christmas paper, throw out boxes, and take down a few of the decorations.

Then I tackle the tree.

I'm halfway through seeking out the end of the Christmas lights when the front door clicks.

"Hello?" James calls from the hallway.

"In here!"

James appears in the doorway with two coffees balanced in a carton in one hand and a bag in the other. "I brought coffee and strudel because I heard you were trying to tidy up, so I thought you would need the energy boost."

"How thoughtful," I reply with a smile. "Any chance you could hold this for me?" I offer out the tail end of the lights, and when James sets aside his gifts and takes it, I begin my investigation of every bulb as we slowly unwind the lights from the tree.

"Aren't these supposed to be off when you remove them?" James asks.

"Technically," I murmur, eyes down on the bulbs. "But this way, I can find all the broken ones *as* I unpack and then I don't have to deal with this impossible tangle more than once."

"It's part of the Christmas magic." James laughs. "Christmas lights will always end up tangled like a nest. I'm pretty sure it's some sort of law laid down by Santa."

"Oh, really?" I shoot him a glance. "Then I want a word with Santa."

"I'll try and arrange that," James says. Suddenly, his warm hand encloses around my wrist and he pulls me away from the tree.

I stumble close to him and place one hand on his chest. "James, I'm trying to work here."

"I know," he murmurs, bringing his face close to mine. "I only want to say hi."

A bashful smile creeps across my lips, followed by a rush of warmth through my entire body as his lips press against mine. Despite everything, James still has an uncanny ability to make me feel like the only woman in the world. I drape my arms around his neck and pull him closer, deepening the kiss.

James reacts in kind and we slowly begin to rotate. He kisses me deeply with his tongue teasing over the seam of my lips before easing into my mouth. Another curl of heat runs through me, and I stroke through the finer hairs at the back of his neck. When the kiss breaks, James begins humming a soft Christmas tune and swaying me back and forth.

Laughing, I go with it and allow him to twirl me around as he hums because after each spin, he pulls me back against him and kisses me deeply. My heart flutters with a mind of its own and I'm utterly smitten until a strange restriction catches around my ankles.

I overbalance with a yelp and would have hit the floor had James not been there to catch me. He holds me in his arms, almost parallel to my arms, laughing heartily. Glancing down, I see that all of his spinning and weaving has tangled me up in the glittering Christmas lights and now I look like some kind of ornate deer.

"Oh, my God," I laugh. "Hold on, help me up."

"Hmm," James hums. "I don't think I will."

"Wait, what?"

The next thing I know, he's got me on the floor and is kissing me deeply as he winds the remainder of the lights around my wrists and pins them just above my head, using the table leg to hold me in place.

It's not very secure, all things given, but I choose to keep my hands there as he kisses me deeply and slides his hands over my abdomen.

"Time for my Christmas gift," James murmurs against my lips.

"The scarf and mug weren't enough?" I gasp when he breaks the kiss. His lips trail down my jaw, and he buries his face into the side of my neck with a groan while his hands slide up my body and grope my breasts through my shirt.

"They were perfect," he murmurs, and his lips tickle my throat as he talks. "But you're better."

I can't argue with that. Curling my hands into loose fists, I grip the cable of the lights and close my eyes. Heat flushes inside me like a furnace, flaring each time James's lips press against my skin.

He lavishes attention down my neck, nibbles across my collar bone, and tears my shirt open to expose my breasts. I don't care about the buttons I hear clattering into the distance. They can be a problem for later.

Right now, James is kissing my breasts and drawing my nipple into his mouth. Flesh stiffens immediately, and I gasp softly, arching into the flush of pleasure that flares from where his tongue swirls in circles around my nipple. There's a flash of teeth and his tongue soothes the area immediately after.

I squirm and giggle when his hands skim over my ribs, and James chuckles with me, then he shoves a hand beneath my leggings, and I'm briefly blinded by the surge of pleasure that courses through me when he slides his fingers over my pussy.

Two slide deep inside me, slicked by the dampness that formed between my legs the moment he pulled me close. I moan loudly, aching to touch him, but the Christmas lights limit my movements and I don't want to break them. James kisses down over my abdomen, teasing my navel, and then he vanishes from sight.

There's a moment when he rolls me back and forth in order to get my leggings and underwear off my legs, and then he buries his face against my pussy, pressing firmly between my barely parted thighs.

My eyes roll back in my head and a rush of tingles shoots through my body as his tongue delves against my core, pumping his fingers inside me with purpose. Then he crooks his digits and his fingertips press against something inside me that sends a sharp pulse of pleasure straight to my core. I jolt with a gasp and writhe on the floor.

"Fuck, James," I gasp, clenching and unclenching my hands. "Holy fuck—fuck!"

He brings me to orgasm in record time, and he doesn't pause his onslaught of attention until I'm a quivering, gasping mess and each swipe of his tongue is like torture.

"You have no idea how beautiful you look," James says once he's discarded his clothes and returned to my side. "All flushed and aroused with the multicolored lights on your skin. A work of art."

"You sweet talker," I moan, nuzzling into him. Above us, the remaining lights on the tree wink down at us from their nest of tinsel.

"It's because I want to fuck you," James teases.

"What are you waiting for?"

I get my answer in his touch. He traces my lips with his thumb, then slides his fingertips over my jaw to my throat. Down my neck to my shoulder, then across the swell of each of my breasts with a light touch to my throbbing nipples, James traces all of me. I feel oddly exposed under the intensity of his gaze, and yet there's such care in the way he squeezes my breast and then continues his path over my abdomen to my soaked pussy and overheating thighs.

It's like he's mapping out every detail of me for some mental portrait.

"Beautiful," he murmurs again, then he rolls against me and his rock-hard cock presses against my hip.

"Do you want me to beg?" I gasp against his lips. "Because I will." I ache to feel him against me, inside me. I want his pants in my ear, his moans in the air, and his thick cock so deep inside me that it's impossible to tell where I end and he begins.

"That's kinda hot." James grins and our eyes meet. "Beg for my cock, Lily. Tell me how eagerly you want it."

"I don't want it," I moan softly, and my core clenches. "I need it. It's all I can think about. I need to feel your dick spearing me open, sliding so deep that I can feel you with each breath. I need your balls slapping my ass, your hand in my hair, your mouth on my tits. I need you everywhere, and making me wait is cruel—"

He kisses me feverishly, ending my breathless tirade of begging. James thrusts his tongue into my mouth, and I suck eagerly as he pries my thighs apart and situates himself between them. The lights tighten around my limbs, but it's strangely erotic to feel restricted. I'd never been tied up before, but the restraining lights unlock something inside me and I thrust my hips up against James.

"Yes," I moan deeply when the next kiss breaks. "Take me," I beg. "Please, just fuck me already!"

James obliges with a single deep thrust that sheaths himself so deep inside me that all air is punched from my lungs and a strained whimper escapes my kiss-flushed lips.

Yes.

James starts to fuck me immediately, hard and fast, while his mouth kisses and nibbles across my breasts. He keeps one hand against my lightly bound wrists and the other trails over my abdomen, caressing my body as he fucks into me with wild abandon. I have no room for thoughts, only acknowledgment of the rapidly building fire of pleasure deep within my core.

I chant his name over and over as I soar higher and higher, and soon, he fucks my second orgasm out of me with a scream. But he doesn't stop there. He continues to fuck me, rolling me onto my stomach and pulling me up onto my knees, then he re-enters me and pounds with a new, deeper angle.

I'm a complete mess, utterly at the mercy of his thrusts and wandering hands. He praises me constantly, massaging my breasts and sliding one of his hands between my soaked thighs to tease and toy with my clit until I'm quivering apart underneath him. His touch is almost too much for my sensitive body, but that only spurs him on, and by the time James comes inside me, he's fucked a third orgasm out of my exhausted body.

Merry fucking Christmas.

We spend twenty minutes on the floor, utterly spent and exhausted, until James untangles me from the lights and moves me to the couch.

I lie there, exhausted, while he kindly cleans me up with a towel and brews us some fresh coffee. Then we cuddle on the couch under blankets and pick at the strudel he brought.

"Wow," I murmur, slowly licking jam from my fingertips. "That was amazing."

"You were phenomenal," James says, kissing my shoulder.

"I like that." I giggle. "Keep that coming."

He kisses back up my neck, and the warmth that builds between us would surely lure me to sleep if I didn't roll over in his arms and see something strange in his eyes.

Is he... unhappy?

"James?" I cup his face gently. "What's wrong?"

"Nothing. Don't worry about it."

"I'm gonna worry. Did I do something?"

James's eyes widen, then he turns his head into my hand and kisses my palm. "No, babe. No. Not a thing. I was just… thinking."

"About?"

"Well…" He takes a deep breath. "You and Emma and your grandparents have taught me how important a loving, caring family is. And then I think about my own mother and I feel guilty for telling her I'm cutting her off."

"You had good reason," I say softly, studying his face. "Do you regret it?"

"I don't know. Maybe? It was a heat-of-the-moment decision. I don't at all excuse what she did to you or what she has done to me, but she is my mom, y'know?"

I nod slowly. "Do you want my honest opinion?"

He meets my eyes. "Please."

"I think if you want to reach out to her, then you should. But do it because you want to and not because you feel you have to. What she did to me is horrible and I will never forgive her for that, but you did lose your dad. Losing your mom, too, would be a lot to bear."

"I think about that," he says softly. "But I don't know if she will ever change."

"Maybe that's what you need to do," I say, lightly kissing his chin. "Be strong. Lay it out to her and see how she reacts. Then you can choose what to do without carrying that kind of guilt, y'know?"

James nods thoughtfully, then dips his head to kiss me.

"I love you."

"I love you too."

32

JAMES

Meeting my mother for lunch is oddly daunting. When I called to arrange lunch just before New Year's, she was quiet on the phone and accepted immediately. We chose a place that was a few towns over because, in a twist that surprised no one, she was *in the area*. Which was code for her traveling here for Christmas but not making contact.

Which is exactly like her.

I arrive at the cafe first and choose a table at the back, checking the closing time to make sure we don't outstay our welcome. The week between Christmas and New Year's is such a strange one. It's almost like the world is stuck in a time bubble where things are still festive but the magic of anticipation is gone.

I stare out at the world, watching people wander past enjoying the cold weather and the snowy landscape without snowfall for the first time in over a week. There's an odd jump of anticipation within my heart because I'm eager for this to be over so I can go home to my woman and my child.

"James?"

I didn't even hear her enter, but suddenly, my mother is standing next to me, sliding leather gloves from her hands.

"Mother. Can I order you anything?"

"Just some tea, thank you." She takes her seat, and I order a pot of tea for the table. It gives her time to adjust herself and get comfortable in a chair that I'm sure she thinks is beneath her.

By the time the teapot arrives, the red flush on my mother's face has calmed and she gives me a tight smile. "I'm happy you called."

"Seemed like the best thing to do," I reply, focusing on pouring myself some tea. "The last thing I'd want is you turning up announced."

Her cheeks flush at the dig and she clears her throat, spooning sugar into her cup. "I was in the area because your Uncle Arnold has property in the area," she says tightly. "That's all."

"Mmm." I keep my responses curt and drink while she pours. After she's had a few sips of tea, I get right into it. "Listen. I invited you here because I feel like how I left things wasn't entirely fair."

My mother's face floods with relief.

"But," I continue before she can say anything, "cutting you off is very much still on the table."

Her face falls. "Oh, James. How can you say something so cruel?"

"Because I'm angry, Mom. You tried to pay the love of my life to get rid of my child, and you hid all knowledge of it from me. Seven years I have wandered around, missing out on some of the most important steps in my daughter's life, and I will *never* get that back because of you."

My hand shakes as I lower my cup.

"That pain of betrayal goes so deep I don't know if I can ever forgive you, do you understand?"

To my surprise, she merely nods.

"But I said some things when emotions were high, and after Dad..." Sighing, I shake my head. "Anyway. So, I thought we should talk."

"Will you believe me if I tell you I honestly thought I was doing the right thing? I didn't want you to throw your life away for a stranger."

"She wasn't a stranger," I reply tightly. "I loved her back then and I love her now. I have always loved her. I just squashed it down to make you happy, but I'm not doing that anymore. I don't need you plotting my life. I don't need you making choices for me, especially without talking to me first, do you understand?"

Mom nods, and her eyes fill with tears. "You paint me as a monster."

"No." I sigh softly, and my heart clenches at seeing her upset. "Your actions do. Even lately with the constant pressure for me to go back to Bernice, even though you knew I was deeply unhappy. It was like that didn't matter to you. Nothing did other than your reputation."

"You're not wrong," she replies, sniffling. "But it's not what you think. One moment, my life was brilliant. I had everything I wanted. Your father was planning his retirement and we were going to travel the world until we were too old to do anything."

I frown slightly. "I had no idea."

"Well." Mom chuckles. "It was just going to be us. And then one day, he was just... gone." She shakes her head, sending her curls bouncing about her face. "And suddenly, everything was dark and cold, and I felt like I was having to fight tooth and nail for some kind of familiarity. I understand I am overbearing and that I have made terrible choices." She dabs at her eyes. "I have done terrible things to keep this family together, and then after your father died, suddenly, I was all alone."

I didn't expect her to acknowledge her bad choices or the pain she caused, and I'm surprised. She's more aware than I realized. And with that comes another realization. She's lonely. Deeply, painfully lonely. While crafting her perfect world and perfect reputation, she ended up alone with only my father knowing the real her.

And now, he is gone.

"And then losing you?" She closes her eyes briefly. "Is there a colder wake-up call than Christmas alone?"

A stab of guilt lances through my chest and I wince inwardly. It was my first Christmas without my dad, and her first without the two of us. To some, that would be punishment enough.

"I need you to understand that I don't want my life controlled," I say, softening my tone. "I've had to fight to get Lily to trust me again, and I will have to fight even longer to keep proving that to her. But I will do it because I love her, and I want to get to know my daughter and catch up on everything I've missed. And you are still my mother."

She looks at me with heavy, sad eyes.

"You need to stop being so... so *militant* about life and just enjoy it, don't you see, Mom? Dad should have been a wake-up call for you too. He worked himself to death. It was terrible and sudden, but it will hurt us for a long time and I... I don't want that for you. And you shouldn't either."

We talk late into the afternoon, draining several other pots of tea, and I lay out the things over the years that will no longer be acceptable going forward. Thankfully, my mother is open to the idea, and it seems my harsh way of cutting ties with her was the last straw she needed to wake up and realize her poisonous ways.

By the time the bill arrives, we've reached a shaky understanding.

"If you are willing to try," I say as I stand, "then you can be in my life. And if you are willing to work hard, then you will need some magic to make it up to Lily. But the important thing is you have to try."

Mom stands and nods. "I will," she says, and for the first time in memory, her smile seems to reach her eyes. "I will change. I promise, James. You won't be disappointed."

My arms ache suddenly, then I reach out and pull her into a hug. She squeaks in surprise, then melts into the hug with a sigh.

All I can do is ask. I can lay out the path she needs to walk, but she has to walk it herself. My heart lifts slightly and I realize Lily was right. Losing my father *and* my mother in the same year would be too much.

"We will both do it," I say with a calm sigh. "We will work together to be a better mother and son, a better family all around."

Because that is what Lily and Emma deserve.

And I will do everything in my power to be the best man I can be, just for them.

33

LILY

It wouldn't be Evergreen Falls without a burst of snowfall ten minutes after the weatherman assures everyone that it will be clear skies for New Year's.

I walk hand in hand with Emma through town, watching the snow fall gently around us. It catches on my coat and melts into the fabric while Emma dances slightly and does her best to catch the snow with her mitten-clad hands.

James walks a few feet behind us, busy on a phone call with his lawyer.

It's insane how busy this past week has been, and yet at the same time, it feels like no time at all has passed. As we walk toward the inn for the New Year's Eve celebration, my mind replays the events of how we even ended up here.

James's show of love at the town square was the most romantic thing that has ever happened to me, and the sight of him under those lights remains in my mind like a picture-perfect postcard. We have a long way to go in terms of fully trusting one another, given everything we have been through, but we're making a good start.

What matters most to me is Emma, and James has doted on her every second. She's taken the news well that he's her father, but I'm braced just in case that changes. If it does, I know we will tackle it together. A few months ago, I never could have imagined such a perfect end to the year. The auction was a roaring success, the free clinic was funded, and James came back to me with a promise to stay.

A promise I believe.

My heart is full and each step is like walking on air. Nothing can take this smile from my face.

"Look, Mommy!" Emma yells excitedly as we reach the inn. She's managed to catch a large snowflake in her hand and for a few seconds, it remains perfectly in shape. Then, the warmth from her mitten causes it to melt and it vanishes into nothing.

"Aww." Emma pouts, dejected, then she flashes me a bright smile and goes right back to trying to catch another.

"Alright!" James puffs out his cheeks and jogs to catch up with us. When he reaches me, he slides his arm around my waist and pulls me close, planting a cold-lipped kiss on my equally cold cheek.

"All sorted?" I ask, patting his cheek with my other hand.

"Yup. I have to pay my lawyer a chunk more for making him work on New Year's Eve, but it's worth it. The trust fund for Emma is set up, and both your names are written into my portion of the estate."

After returning from lunch with his mother, James had the idea. Something about their discussion had prompted him to immediately make sure that Emma and I would be taken care of in the event anything happened to him. It was an incredibly sweet gesture, and a small part of me rests easy knowing that Emma has something waiting for her.

That kind of security for my daughter is priceless.

"I'm sure he doesn't mind." I chuckle softly. "I'd work New Year's Eve for half of what you pay him."

"But then who would come with me to this super-cool party, huh?" James leans in close, and our frost-bitten noses brush against one another. He claims another kiss, and I'd linger if not for Emma slipping free of my grasp.

"Grandma!" She runs full pelt across the snow toward the inn where my mother stands, holding the door open.

"Munchkin!" Upon arrival, she scoops Emma up into her arms and they spin together as Emma immediately begins to tell her, in great detail, about every snowflake she caught on the way here.

"There's one more thing," James says as we wander after Emma.

"A good thing?" I ask.

"Yup. I've set up a fund for the clinic too."

"What?" I stop dead in the snow. "What kind of fund?"

"A charitable one. It will be placed on donation lists for anyone eager to make themselves look good by donating to a clinic."

"Oh, my God!" Leaping upward, I throw my arms around his shoulders and hug him close. "That's amazing!"

"You don't mind?" He laughs, cuddling me back.

"Hell no! If some rich tosspot wants to make themselves feel better by donating a crap-ton to our clinic, then I'll happily accept their money. It will help people. That's all that matters."

"I knew you'd be happy." James grins. He kisses me slowly, tucking a loose strand of hair behind my ear as he does so.

"Thank you."

With a final kiss, we head inside to the New Year's party that's already in full swing. Emma runs off to play with her friends, and my dad presses drinks into both of our hands, assuring us that a room has been set up for us whenever we decide to crash.

Most of the town is here, squashed into the event hall, and everyone is in good spirits. Alcohol flows, music fills the air, and we all dance while sharing stories about the year. I pass Amelia, who has her lips locked onto a handsome man whose name I will find out later. She waggles her brows at me in greeting and then resumes kissing the face off her date. Everyone else we pass talks about James's presentation in the square, telling us that we make such a beautiful couple.

To my surprise, James's mother is here. I hadn't expected her to accept my invitation, but seeing her amid the townsfolk, she really does stand out. But she has a drink in her hand and a smile on her face, and while she has a lot of making up to do for both of us, James assures me that giving her a chance is the right thing to do. But she only gets one. Given what happened to his father, I support him, and we greet her warmly as we pass.

Two dances later, we run into Margret who scolds James slightly for adding years to her face when she wasn't sure if he would come back or not. James promises to make it all up to her next year.

We drink and we dance, sometimes with Emma and sometimes by ourselves. James has as much coordination on the dancefloor as he does on the ice, but his heart is in it and we laugh together all night long.

This is my happily ever after.

On one particular twirl, James sends me out from his body, and I close my eyes, soaking up the atmosphere and the warmth of James's hand entangled with my own.

But when I spin back, my heart screeches to a halt.

James is no longer standing. Instead, he kneels in the doorway next to us right under a fat clump of mistletoe, and something huge sparkles in his eyes.

"Marry me, Lily."

The crowd around us goes deathly silent as more and more people notice James down on one knee. Emma squeals in delight and is immediately scooped up by my father.

"Marry me," James repeats as I stare at him, rooted to the floor in absolute shock. "I know it's fast. In fact, it might feel insanely fast, but I have loved you for seven years, and I have missed so much. Too much. All that wasted time is time I am desperate to make up for, and I swear to you, I will. I will spend every single day loving you, Lily. And loving Emma. And I will make sure you know it, every single day."

I can't breathe. My heart beats so wildly, it's like roaring in my ears, and I clutch at my chest.

"So marry me," James says with tears sparkling in his eyes. "Do me the incredible honor of becoming my wife."

Is this real? I almost want to pinch myself, but I'm too scared to move in case this is some odd dream.

The room is silent, and James stares up at me with such open, honest hope in his eyes.

"Yes!" I gasp as tears flood my eyes and my heart pounds like a drum. "A thousand times, yes!"

Trembling, I hold out my hand as cheers of delight rise from the crowd behind me. James slides the sparkling ring onto my finger, then he surges up and gathers me in his arms, spinning me around as he peppers kisses all over my face.

There's no doubt here. He is the man I want to spend the rest of my life with, and while I'd never given much thought to marriage, I'm never more sure of anything than saying yes in that moment.

We kiss repeatedly as he spins me around, and then, just outside the windows, the dark night sky explodes with colors as multiple fireworks race into the sky and explode.

"A little early!" I hear my dad laughing in the crowd.

I don't care. The explosions of color dance across James's face as he kisses me deeply, cradling my face like I'm the most precious thing he's ever held. We're joined a few seconds later by Emma who comes flying through the crowd and tackles our legs.

"Yay!" she yells. "Mommy and Daddy together!"

James scoops her up into his arms and balances her against his hip, then he slides his other hand around my waist and repeatedly kisses my cheek.

I'm about to speak, but out of the crowd melts his mother, and a pulse of apprehension tightens across my shoulders. I brace for whatever she has to say.

"You make a beautiful couple," she says with a small smile. Then she takes my hand, pressing a small, cold object into my palm. As she releases me, I spot a small gold brooch with their family name woven across the plaque.

"Welcome to the family, Lily."

It's a small gesture at the start of a very long road to forgiveness, so I smile at her the best I can.

"Thank you. I appreciate this a lot."

She nods and disappears back into the crowd as James moves us closer to the window. Together, we watch the too-early fireworks display light up the night sky.

"I love you, Lily," James says, kissing my cheek again and again.

"I love you too."

"And I love *you!*" James buries his face in Emma's neck, making her squeal and giggle.

"I promise we will never be apart again," he says, and I turn to look him in the eyes.

"You promise?"

"I promise," he swears. "This is the first of a lifetime of Christmases and New Years together. Until we're old and gray."

I cup his face and bring him into a deep, slow kiss as my heart overflows with love.

Until we are old and gray.

Printed in Great Britain
by Amazon